HE SAID, SHE SAID,

"MURDER"

Book One

By

Jeramy Gates

Published by Timber Hill Press

Other exciting titles by

Jeramy Gates:

He said, She said "Murder" series

Valkyrie Smith mystery/thriller series

Erased, a thriller

The Vigilante Killer (short story)

Hank Mossberg, Private Ogre
(Fantasy/Detective Series written as Jamie Sedgwick)

Chapter 1

Tanja Shepherd
(Prologue)

The thought of Joe following the killer into that creepy old building sent a chill crawling down my spine. I used the sleeve of my jacket to wipe the fog from the car window and gazed across the dark parking lot at the dilapidated old warehouse where my husband had disappeared. The rain came down in sheets. Lightning flashed, the light glinting in the blacked-out windows, the ominous rumble of thunder echoing up and down the coastal mountains.

"Give me fifteen minutes," Joe had said, "If I'm not back by then, drive down the road until you get a phone signal. Call Sheriff Diekmann."

Joe's plan had two problems: First, it was storming violently, and the odds that I'd get a cell signal anywhere along the Sequoia coast on a night like that were somewhere between nil and none. Even in clear weather, cell reception on the NorCal coast comes and goes at will. For all I knew, a cell tower may have been half a mile away. Tucked into a narrow valley between the coast and the cliffs, with the wind howling off the bay and the rain pounding down, it may as well have been a hundred miles.

The second problem was that Joe had the car keys *in his pocket*. I hadn't even noticed that little tidbit of information until after he was gone. I didn't have a spare, and hot-wiring the Suburban didn't seem like the best alternative, especially since we still had three years of payments left to make. I simultaneously wanted to call him a moron for leaving me in that predictament, and felt an aching dread in my chest for his safety.

I glanced at my cell phone and confirmed that I still had zero bars. I opened the center console and pulled out my 9mm Glock. I checked the magazine to make sure it was loaded. I patted my swollen belly.

"Looks like it's just you and me, baby Autumn. Time to rescue daddy again."

Chapter 2

One week earlier:

My name is Tanja Shepherd. It's the traditional German spelling, with a "J" instead of a "Y." It seems to throw some people off, especially during those sales calls I get from some anonymous stranger hundreds -or thousands- of miles away, who insists on pronouncing it like "jam" instead of "yam" no matter how many how times I correct him. It's really annoying. Tanja does *not* rhyme with ganja. Period.

I suppose the unusual spelling of my name makes me strange to some people, but certainly no stranger than the fact that I'm six feet tall and several inches taller than my husband. That definitely throws some people off. We get looks. Most of the time, I can guess what people are thinking as they size us up. They glance at my husband Joe, they notice his broad shoulders, his shaved head and goatee, and then they look at me, the six-foot blonde, and it's obvious that something brought us together. Not just physical attraction, although it is definitely there, but something deeper; some connection based on our personalities and experiences that you can't quantify in mechanical, physical terms.

Usually, they conclude that we're just two unique people who found one another attractive and fell in love. Other times, they don't. I see the smirk beginning to form, the slow curl at the edge of the lip, the amused gaze that lingers just a little too long. It's funny to them, as if a couple inches of difference in height made us two completely different species. Beyond the obvious, I really can't guess what's going on in their minds, but I don't expect it's much. It doesn't make me self-conscious, because it says more about them than it does about us. Joe and I are happy, and that's what matters.

There is one last thing, one more unusual detail about the two of us: Joe and I are private detectives. It wasn't always that way. We used to be cops. Joe worked undercover and I was an FBI behavior analyst. I'll explain more on that later. Long story short: we ended up in Sequoia County with a baby on the way and hardly a penny in the bank. That is, until Sheriff Diekmann suggested we go into business. That wasn't working out so well, but then he came up with another proposition.

It was a sunny January morning, and I had just started a pot of coffee when I heard the doorbell ring. I stepped out of the kitchen as Joe came wandering down the hall, drying his freshly shaved head with a hand towel. I opened the door to see Sheriff Diekmann standing there with a wrinkled cardboard box.

"Morning," he said with a nod. "Do you and Joe have a few minutes?"

The sheriff had heavy bags under his eyes and more crow's feet and wrinkles than an old paper bag. His dark brown hair was slightly mussed, curling up around the telltale ring of an old baseball cap he usually wears. He needed a shave too, but that's pretty much how Bill Diekmann looks all the time. He's the kind of man who owns just one suit: a black one, reserved especially for funerals. The rest of the time, he wears faded jeans, flannel shirts, and the aforementioned cap.

I invited him in of course, and we gathered in the kitchen. Diekmann set the box next to the table, and I poured him a cup of coffee. After we had settled, he explained the reason for his unexpected visit.

"Sorry to drop in on you," he said. "I've heard the two of you might be looking for work. I think I can help with that."

Looking for work? That was an understatement. It was just a few weeks after Joe and I had launched our business, and we hadn't had a single client. Still, I was a bit hesitant about the idea of working for the sheriff. Working with friends can be a recipe for trouble, and I didn't know the sheriff as well as Joe. I had barely lived in Sequoia County for a year.

"I know this isn't the kind of job you have done before," he said. "You won't be chasing down bad guys and having wild shootouts. In these cases, the bad guys are long gone and the trail has gone cold, if there ever was one. All that's left is to clean up the mess. In most cases, you probably won't even be able to do that."

He leaned back in his chair. "Let me be honest: These are lousy cases, and you probably won't be able to solve most of them. But the department is willing to pay you on a case by case basis, if you can produce results. I wish I could do more for you, but those are the terms. It's up to you if you want the job or not."

I fixed my gaze on the manila folder in the sheriff's hand and glanced over at Joe. I found him staring at me, grinning like always, amused by everything. His goatee accentuated his smile. A diffuse ray of sunlight glinted off his freshly shaved head, illuminating the tiny whisker-like hairs that are otherwise invisible.

I don't mind Joe's bald head, but I have explicitly forbidden him to shave his thick blond goatee.

Joe's eyes were deep green that day, like emeralds laced with gold. Sometimes they're blue. They change color with his moods, and when he wears certain clothes. At that moment, they were wordlessly urging me to accept the sheriff's challenge, silently whispering, *"Yes! This is what I've been waiting for!"*

I smiled. I already knew how Joe felt about all of this, how he believed that God and the universe had just handed us this opportunity right when we needed it most. He's always held the conviction that everything in the world happens for a reason. Joe finds life fascinating, the ups and downs, the inexplicable things that happen, the synchronicity of it all. Sometimes I think it's all a game to him.

I glanced back at the sheriff, who was still waiting for our answer.

"Absolutely," I said with all the confidence I could muster. "When Joe and I started this business, we knew it would be tough to get off the ground. We need the work, and we're more than happy to help out."

"Glad to hear it."

The sheriff opened a folder and produced half a dozen snapshots, which he spread out across the kitchen table. "I'd like you to start with this case, if you don't mind." He selected a photo and handed it to me. It was a girl in her late teens with shoulder-length chestnut hair and dark, almond shaped eyes. It was an outdoor shot, probably taken by a friend. She was leaning up against a Camaro, smiling and pretty... happy, like any girl that age should be. I showed the image to Joe.

"Pretty girl," I said. "She seems very happy."

"That's the victim, Becky Sweet," the sheriff said. "She was murdered five years ago. She was a senior at

10

Healdsburg High School. Her father had committed suicide several years before that, and for a while, Becky's mother was afraid she was becoming suicidal. The two of them went through an intensive counseling program together.

"When it was all over, Becky seemed to have recovered. She became a cheerleader and a high school teen counselor. She had lots of friends, and seemed to be loved by everyone. It really rattled the community when she was murdered."

"What happened to her?" said Joe.

"She was drowned." The sheriff grimaced as he produced another photo. He handed it to me, and I looked it over. I saw a large room with a concrete floor and several rows of stainless steel tanks. In the foreground was a sheet-covered body lying on the floor. Puddles and splatters of white fluid covered the area. Nothing else leapt out at me.

"What is this place?" I said.

"Timber Hills Dairy Farm. It's just a couple miles south of Vine Hill."

Joe snatched the photo out of my hand. "Are you saying Becky was drowned in *milk*?"

"Cream, to be exact," said the sheriff. "When the owner showed up for work that morning, she found Becky's body in one of those vats. Apparently, the cream had been run through a separator and left over-night in a vat. Someone shoved her in there, and then sealed the lid."

"You're sure this couldn't have been accidental?" I said.

"Unlikely. The coroner determined that the killer struck Becky from behind with a wrench and dumped her into the cream. The weapon was found at the scene.

We found D.N.A. under her fingernails, but it didn't match anything on record. We didn't recover any prints."

"Did Becky work at the dairy?" Joe said.

"No, the dairy owner had never seen her before. At the time, there was only one other employee, a mentally disabled man. He's the one who found the body. Traumatized him pretty bad, too. Becky's mother had reported her missing the night before, so it didn't take long to confirm her identity."

We fell silent, all three of us staring at the grisly photo.

"What about a motive?" I said. "Are there any suspects?"

Diekmann picked up one of the other photos and handed it to me. It was a mug shot of teenage male with shoulder-length dark brown hair and a sleeveless t-shirt with the logo of a band called *Death Metal*. He looked like a run of the mill troublemaker. His eyes were very angry, but his face was almost expressionless. I looked closer, and noticed a purple bruise on his left shoulder, right below the tattoo of a skull with a snake looping through the eye sockets.

"That's Jimmy Pishard Junior," Diekmann said. "He was our prime suspect at the time. He had been dating Becky, and they'd just had a nasty breakup. His only alibi for the night of her disappearance was that he'd fallen asleep watching TV after getting high. He was alone."

"No alibi," Joe said. "It sounds to me like an open and shut case."

"We thought so, too. Unfortunately, we couldn't find anything solid to pin it on him. The few pieces of

D.N.A. evidence we found weren't a match. We had nothing to place him at the scene."

"What kind of D.N.A. did you have?" I asked.

"The skin under her nails, and we found a spot of blood on the vat."

The sheriff handed me another photo, this one of a tall, thin man in his forties with graying hair and a permanent scowl etched onto his face. "That's James Pishard Senior, Jimmy's father. He couldn't vouch for Jimmy, because he was out of town for a business convention. In fact, he took one of our investigators aside during the interview and told him he didn't trust his son. James even said that he wouldn't be surprised if Jimmy *had* killed Becky."

"Why would he say something like that?" I said. "Did Jimmy have a history of violence?"

"No, we ran a full background check and came up with zip. We even interviewed a few of his teachers and they had nothing bad to say about him. If you read the notes, the detectives didn't buy it. They were sure Jimmy was into some sort of trouble, and that made him the prime suspect."

"Why's that?" said Joe.

"I don't know, intuition maybe. He had outright admitted to smoking pot. Then there was his hair and all."

"Meaning what?" I said curiously.

The sheriff leaned back in his chair and laced his fingers behind his head. "When a kid looks like that, and as much as admits he's involved with drugs, it tends to put the spotlight on him. Between the long hair, the drugs, and the heavy metal music, you can imagine why they suspected him. Not to mention the fact that he lived just two miles away from where the body was discovered."

"Everybody in Vine Hill lives two miles away from where the body was discovered," Joe said with a chuckle.

I glanced at the photos of Jimmy and his father, wondering what could drive such a wedge between a man and his son. Clearly, there was a lot more to the story. I took a good look at James. The man appeared very stern, very proud... but was he violent? I know the symptoms of an abusive relationship from both training and experience, and I would have bet my last dollar that James Pishard had been abusing his son. Jimmy had been rebelling against something, and I had a strong feeling it was his father. This dark dynamic in their relationship piqued my curiosity. I couldn't help wondering if it had something to do with Becky's disappearance.

"So what happened?" said Joe. "Did you press charges?"

The sheriff folded his hands on the table. "We didn't have much on Jimmy at the time, but we wanted to make sure he didn't skip the state. The D.A. was sure he could make a case. Then the D.N.A. evidence fell through, and the D.A. ended up dropping the charges rather than face double jeopardy sometime down the road."

"So that was the end of it?" I said.

"There wasn't anything else to do. My deputies interviewed Becky's friends, the other cheerleaders, her teachers... we couldn't come up with any other suspects..." he displayed his empty hands. "We had nothing."

Joe asked to see the file, and quietly thumbed through the pages. "There's not much here. A few interviews, some observations by your investigators. I can see why this case was never solved."

"I had given up on it," said the sheriff. "Which is tragic, because Becky deserves better than that. So does her mother. Kendra Sweet fell apart. You can imagine what it was like for her, after her husband's suicide, and then her daughter's death. Unfortunately, we didn't have the funds or manpower to keep pursuing a dead end, and that's what this case turned out to be. That is, unless you can find something we missed."

"Says her car went missing, too," Joe said, stroking his goatee. "It's kind of hard to hide a whole car, isn't it? Especially a sixty-nine Camaro."

"We listed the car as stolen and posted a statewide B.O.L.O. Never heard a word. That car just vanished into thin air."

Joe set the file on the table and looked up with a smile. "Thanks for everything, sheriff. We'll get right on this. We'll find your man and deliver him in cuffs."

"As cocky as ever, I see."

"Worse than ever," I said.

I pushed away from the table, making room for my belly as I rose from the chair. The sheriff glanced at the basketball-sized lump under my shirt and smiled.

"Do you know what the baby's going to be?"

"A girl," I said proudly. "Joe's a little freaked out, but I couldn't be happier."

"I'm not freaked out," Joe said, feigning hurt. "I just don't know what you're supposed to *do* with a baby girl. Boys are easy. They make forts, climb trees, ride skateboards..."

"You never know," said the sheriff. "I've seen girls do all that. Have you settled on a name?"

Joe and I exchanged a smile. "We named our business after her," I said. "Autumn's Hope Detective Agency."

"Autumn, then," said the sheriff. "Nice name, on both counts."

"We thought it made sense," said Joe. "Considering this business is Autumn's only hope of ever getting into college."

The sheriff threw his head back and laughed. "I'm sure you'll do just fine."

He headed for the door, and Joe followed him. I could hear their voices fading into the distance as Joe accompanied Diekmann out to his truck. I waited until they were nearly to the street before I walked across the kitchen and opened the drawer under the coffee pot.

I stared at the envelope in the bottom of the drawer for a moment before taking it out. I had left it in there all weekend, ever since it had arrived in the mail Friday afternoon. I'd hidden it away from Joe, not out of dishonesty, but because I was waiting for the right time to show it to him. Unfortunately, that time had yet to come. I was beginning to wonder if it ever would.

Honestly, I didn't have the heart to show it to him. That was the problem. Joe had sacrificed so much for us already, for our family. I didn't know how to break it to him. I opened the enveloped and carefully unfolded the letter inside. I stared at the big, bold print at the top of the page that read:

"Past Due Notice: You are in danger of foreclosure!"

I heard the sheriff's truck start up out front. I jammed the letter into the envelope and shoved it back in the drawer. By the time Joe had returned, I had settled back down at the table. I didn't say a word as he sat down next to me.

Chapter 3

Joe

I sensed that Sheriff Diekmann had something on his mind, so I walked him out to his truck.
Tanja must have picked up on it too, because instead of joining us, she stayed in the house to study Becky's file.

It was a bright sunny morning, and the warm weather had done my leg some good. I didn't bother grabbing my cane on the way out. As we approached Diekmann's truck, I glanced at the park across the street. It was a field of green, glistening with moisture, the redwood grove behind it dark and impenetrable. The scene was a perfect metaphor for Sequoia County: beautiful, refined, even alluring at first glance, but dark and mysterious, filled with secrets upon closer inspecttion.

Diekmann and I walked in silence until we reached his old Dodge truck. He opened the door, grabbed his baseball cap off the dash, and turned to face me with a serious look as he put it on. He propped his elbow up through the open window, looking more like a farmer than a county sheriff.

"How are *things,* Joe?" he said.

I smiled suspiciously. "Things are fine, Bill. Why?"

He averted his gaze, staring at a car crossing the intersection a few blocks down the street. "I talked to your grandmother the other day. She's worried about you."

18

"She's always worried," I said. "Don't take her too seriously. We'll be all right. Before you know it, we'll be so busy we'll have to turn down cases."

"I'm not talking about your business. I'm talking about *you*."

I shifted uncomfortably. "What about me?"

"I've heard about what happened to you, when you were working undercover. That sort of thing can affect a man."

I drew my gaze back to the redwoods, wishing I were over there instead of waist deep in this uncomfortable conversation.

"I won't get too personal," Diekmann continued. "I just want to make sure you're okay. We have a therapist you could talk to. Don't worry about the fee, the department will take care of it."

"Thanks for the offer," I said, "but it's really not necessary."

"I understand. I just wanted you to know." He dug in his pocket until he managed to find his wallet, and produced a business card. "Just in case. If you ever feel like you need somebody to talk to... sometimes it helps to tell those stories."

I accepted the card and gave him a devious smile. "I don't remember you being such a pushover, sheriff. You must be getting soft in your old age."

"Maybe," he said. He grunted as he climbed into his truck. He pulled the door shut and leaned out the window. "Maybe I'm just sick and tired of seeing what P.T.S.D. does to people I care about."

"You've got nothing to worry about. Tell granny to quit snitching on me."

He laughed. "All right. You just keep that card. Give me a call if you have any luck with the case."

"Will do, sheriff."

He drove off and I stood there a minute, watching after him until his truck disappeared. I looked down at the card and thought of Grandma. I hadn't seen her in almost a month. I made up my mind to pay her a visit.

Back inside the house, I found Tanja studiously examining Diekmann's file. She didn't seem happy. I settled down across the table from her, admiring the way the morning sunlight set off the highlights in her hair. She raised her gaze to meet mine, and I found myself lost in her hazel eyes. They were greener than usual, and I felt like I could stare into them all day. It was not to be so. She sighed deeply, and said:

"Diekmann's paperwork is a joke."

I winced. "This isn't the FBI You know that, right?"

She grabbed a page and started reading. *"Lindsey Garcia – Becky's BFF – nice girl. Suspects Jimmy – Bad Breakup...* Seriously, Joe? This is what they call an investigation around here? Other than her name, I don't know anything about this girl. There's no contact information, no relationship... it doesn't even specify that she goes to the same school!"

"The investigators probably didn't take many notes because they already knew most of these kids. Half the people in this county are related to each other."

"That's no excuse for shoddy police work," she grumbled.

"Don't be too hard on the locals. They're good cops, they just don't have the training we do. We can't all be perfect like you."

Tanja snorted. "Ha, nobody's perfect. It doesn't hurt to *try,* though."

"Look at it like this: If they were *more* perfect, we might be out of a job."

She snickered. I began thumbing through the photographs. "I know you well enough by now to know that you've figured out something from these pictures. What does your body language and psychology training tell you about this kid? Is Jimmy the real killer, or not?"

I produced another photo of the suspect from the pile. This was a personal photo. His hair dangled down over his shoulders, and he was staring sullenly into the camera lens, as if he had too many things on his mind to smile. He was with friends, hanging out in a parking lot somewhere. He was smoking a cigarette. He wore a beaded necklace that looked like native American jewelry. I couldn't make out the design... it was possibly a thunderbird.

Tanja frowned, staring at the image of the teen.

"His body language is open, but reserved," she said. "Notice how he appears relatively at ease, leaning back against the car, but his legs are crossed? Even among friends, he keeps his upper body twisted slightly to the side, and his eyes are downcast. All signs of introversion and defensiveness. I doubt he's the killer, but I would need to meet him to be sure."

"The investigators were sure it was him."

"Because of his hair, Joe. Seriously?"

"And the drugs."

"Uh-huh. Drugs that are now legal in California, and half a dozen other states. I'm not going to make any assumptions about this kid. Especially not based on what those investigators thought."

"All right," I said. "I guess we'll have to interview him for ourselves."

21

Tanja turned on her laptop and ran a quick internet search. According to PeopleStalker.com, Jimmy Pishard, Jr. lived at a farm just outside of town.

"That was easy," I said. "Shall we pay him a visit?"

Tanja glanced at the clock. "I suppose we might as well get started. The sooner we find the killer, the sooner we get paid."

"Good attitude," I said, and grabbed the Suburban keys.

The address was in the hills north of Vine Hill. The paved road quickly gave way to gravel and potholes, and I hit one of them hard before I realized how bad they were.

"Joe!" Tanja gasped, clutching her belly as we went bouncing across the road. "Slow down!"

"Sorry." I eased back on the accelerator and took the rest of the drive at a crawl. It took fifteen minutes to drive a little over one mile.

Near the end of the road, we found a mailbox with the address we were looking for. I turned onto the steep, awkwardly twisting driveway and Tanja twisted her face up as she grabbed the roof handle.

"Hang on," I said.

Thankfully, it wasn't far. A hundred yards up the hill, the road leveled out and I parked in front of an old yellow farmhouse with faded, peeling paint and several missing pieces of siding. There was an old cedar barn standing in the background, and a scattering of rusty old farm equipment buried in weeds all around the property. A vineyard crawled up the steep hill behind the barn.

As we stepped out of the Suburban, a man's voice shouted, "No Jehovahs!" I traced the sound to a shadowy figure sitting in a rocker at the far end of the porch. Tanja and I exchanged a glance.

"Perhaps you can help us," she called out. "We're looking for Jimmy Pishard."

There was a shuffling noise as the man rose from his chair and came forward to the handrail. He was elderly, probably in his early seventies. He had thick white hair, long silver whiskers, and liver spots on his face and arms. He was wearing a pair of overalls and a stained brown t-shirt that may have once been white.

"You cops?" he said suspiciously.

"No," said Tanja. "We're journalists. We're doing a piece on unsolved mysteries. What was your name?"

"Mel Colson. What can I do to help you?" He stepped around the post and came down the stairs. Tanja reached into the Suburban and pulled out a notepad. I suppressed a grin as she started jotting something down.

"Mel Colson," she repeated, as he sauntered up to us. "Mr. Colson, are you familiar with Jimmy Pishard?"

He scratched his whiskers. "Yep, sure am. He rented a space from me a while back. Interesting sort, that one."

"Why is that?"

"Oh, he was real quiet. Kinda shy. Didn't talk to the other workers. Was always back in his room, reading or watching TV."

"He worked for you?"

"Here and there. Helped out with the vineyard, did some odd jobs. When the season ended, I sent him on his way. I don't mind payin' gringos if they can work, but this ain't a hotel."

"I see," Tanja said, apparently noting down everything he said in her notebook. "And when exactly was this?"

The farmer spit a big brown puddle of tobacco juice on the dirt between his tattered leather boots. Some of it dribbled down his chin, and he wiped it on the back of his sleeve. "Two years, I reckon."

Tanja noted the answer. "Do you know where we could find him now?"

"Sorry, cain't help you. When I said it was time, he was gone, lickety-split. I got a policy about vagrants."

"I see. Well thank you, Mr. Colson. I'll be sure to acknowledge you when our story is published."

"That's C-O-L-S-O-N," he said helpfully.

"Got it," Tanja said, smiling. We climbed back into the Suburban. Halfway down the drive, we both broke out laughing.

"Unbelievable," she said. "I've never seen anybody like that in real life. He was like a character from a reality TV show."

"Brace yourself," I said. "The woods are crawling with them. I bet he had fifty pot plants growing out behind that barn."

"I'm surprised you didn't try to arrest him."

"Very funny. First of all, I'm not a cop anymore, and second, what would be the point? There are a thousand pot farms between here and the Oregon border. If I turn in a person like that, I just make room for some hardcore drug operation to take his place. Besides, for all we know, the guy might be licensed by the state."

Tanja tossed the notepad on the dash. I glanced at it, and saw that she hadn't written down a single thing.

"How did you come up with that, anyway? Pretending to be a reporter?"

"It was off the top of my head. I was thinking novelist at first, but that didn't make sense because there were two of us. Novelists work alone. Journalists made more sense."

"How did you know it would work?"

She stared at me. "You do remember what I do for a living, right?"

"Amazing. It took you ten seconds to realize he'd open up for a couple of reporters. But why not just tell him that we're private investigators?"

"Nope, not that guy. He won't talk to cops, investigators, or even Jehovah's Witnesses. He probably chases off the insurance appraiser with a shotgun."

"Well played," I said. "Unfortunately, it sounds like Jimmy Pishard has gone off the grid. How are we going to find him now?"

"Let's try his father. According to the website records, James Pishard, Sr. owns a boat dealership in Santa Rosa. With any luck, he'll still be there."

"Sounds good."

"But Joe, one thing first."

"What's that?"

"Find me a bathroom."

Santa Rosa is a small city about 15 miles south of Vine Hill and fifty miles north of San Francisco. Zoning laws restrict any building larger than four stories, which creates a deceptive small town atmosphere, but also forces the city's ever-growing population to expand outward rather than upward. Combine that with the amount of Sequoia real estate already tied up in vineyards, and you have a recipe for sky-high property prices. Sometimes, I'm amazed at the number of people who can afford to live there.

25

I stopped at a gas station on the way to Santa Rosa. After Tanja had relieved her uncomfortably compressed bladder, we headed for the highway. Traffic was light. Fifteen minutes later, I took the exit in south Santa Rosa and cruised down the narrow lane, moving south on Auto Row past a dozen different new and used car dealers. At the very end of the road, I found the place we were looking for. It was a large single story building with a banner hanging from the roof that said, "Sequoia Marine Sports."

I hadn't even locked the doors before a salesman pounced on us. He was in his early forties, balding and thirty pounds overweight. I noted flashes of gold on his fingers and around his throat. *Dress for success,* the old adage says. *If you look successful, you will be.* I had a feeling this guy repeated that mantra in his sleep.

He gave us a beaming smile as he approached us, and I noticed his gaze lingering on my wife. Normally, sizing up a man's pregnant wife is just asking for trouble, but I ignored it. Tanja has that effect on men. She's a tall curvy blonde with amazing hazel eyes and an athletic build that even in her late stage of pregnancy was hard not to notice. Besides, even in her condition, I knew Tanja could drop the guy in about two seconds if she wanted to.

"I'm Shane," he said, smiling as he reached out to shake my hand, a mouthful of perfect pearly whites gleaming like something out of a toothpaste commercial. "What can I show you today? We've got the biggest selection of boats in the north bay. We're exclusive dealers for several popular lines. Are you looking to upgrade, or is this your first boat?"

"Actually, we're looking for James Pishard," Tanja said. "Is he available?"

Shane's face fell. He'd been hoping for a sale, and since it was February, he probably needed one bad. He recovered instantly, though. The smile was right back in place.

"Sure thing, I'll grab him for you. Feel free to look around."

As he disappeared into the building, Tanja sighed.

"What's the matter?" I said.

"I suppose this is the part where they let us wander around the lot for half an hour, hoping something will catch our eye."

"In that case, I guess we'd better start wandering."

I headed for the front of the lot and Tanja followed me. I was moving with just the slightest pronouncement of a limp. Someone who wasn't paying attention wouldn't even have noticed. I felt a dull ache in my hip and knew a storm was coming, but for the time being, I was fine without my cane.

James arrived fifteen minutes later. Tanja and I were admiring a sleek sailboat with silver racing stripes. *I* was admiring it. She was telling me repeatedly, "It's not going to happen."

"Fine vessel there," James said as he approached us. "I've been eyeing that one myself. I'm James Pishard, the owner."

He was tall and thin with a confident swagger. His hair and eyebrows were the sort of black that only comes in a bottle. He quickly sized up the two of us, observing our clothes, our shoes, our jewelry, anything else that might indicate how much money or credit we had. I also noticed the slight double take he did when he noticed that Tanja is taller than I am. He didn't show an outward sign of this observation, but I'm sure he found it amusing.

"Mr. Pishard," Tanja said. "I'm Tanja Shepherd and this is my husband Joe. We're investigators working with the Sequoia Sherriff's Department. We'd like to ask you a few questions about your son, Jimmy."

Pishard's face darkened, and his smile vanished. "What has the punk done this time?" he said under his breath.

"This is regarding the death of Becky Sweet, five years ago," Tanja said.

"Did you finally get some evidence?"

"I'm not at liberty to discuss the details of our investigation. We need to speak to your son." From the look on Jim's face, he took that as a yes, which was probably just what Tanja had intended.

"I haven't seen him in ages. The last I heard, Jimmy had moved into a trailer up in Fort Bragg. He was working at some junkyard."

"According to our records, you said that you believed Jimmy was capable of murder. Is there any reason for that?"

"The kid's a psychopath." He unbuttoned his shirtsleeve and rolled it up, displaying a long angular scar that ran from just above his wrist to the inner elbow on his left arm. "This is what he did to me before I kicked him out. Came after me with a butcher knife."

"That's frightening," Tanja said. "He could have killed you."

"Would have, if I hadn't knocked him out cold."

"Did this sort of thing happen between the two of you very often?"

Sensing a trap, Jim gave her a cockeyed look. "You mean him attacking me? It happened a couple times, I guess."

"How many times did you beat him, before he fought back?"

Jim went rigid. "I never hurt that kid," he said, curling his lips. "I fed him, clothed him, did all that after his mom left. I provided for him."

"When did your wife leave you?" Tanja said. Jim clenched his jaw, and I saw the muscles bulging on his temples. He stepped forward, a little too close for comfort, and lowered his voice.

"Look lady, I don't know what you're getting at, but you better mind your own business."

I tensed up. I could see that Tanja was pushing him, looking for some sort of reaction, but I couldn't understand why. The man was obviously emotionally unstable. It was dangerous, especially in her condition.

"Did it make you feel strong?" she said.

He reached out, poking his index finger into her shoulder. "Lady, I should-"

"Step back," I said, putting a hand on his arm.

He flinched, jerking away from me, and threw a sucker punch aimed at my nose. I saw the attack coming, and twisted my head to the side. The blow glanced off my ear. I responded with a sharp uppercut that sent him staggering back.

I leapt forward, tackling him, crushing him against the bow of the sailboat. I felt the fiberglass hull buckling under our weight, but I didn't care. I grabbed him by the collar and drove my fist into his face. I drew back and hit him again, and again, and then suddenly became aware of Tanja's cool grip on my arm.

I hesitated. I glanced at her, and she locked gazes with me. My heart was drumming, the rushing sound of blood filling my ears. My lungs burned as I sucked in deep gasps of air. The world around me was silent, motionless. As I stared into her face, the rage slipped away. I remembered who I was, and where I was. I released Pishard and took a step back. He rolled off the boat and landed on his hands and knees.

Slowly, he rose to his feet. He wiped his bleeding nose across the back of his sleeve.

"I'm gonna sue you," he snarled, his body swaying to and fro like a sapling in the wind. "I'm gonna sue you for everything you've got!" He went charging into the building, and disappeared behind the dark, mirror-like windows. We started walking back to the Suburban.

"Well, that could have gone better," Tanja said with a sigh.

"Don't look at me. You started it."

"I know, I meant to ruffle his feathers. I just didn't expect him to turn violent so easily."

"You wanted to tick him off?"

"Yes. Jim just gave us a glimpse into his son's life. Did you see how fast he lost control of his emotions?"

"Uh, yeah. You see this blood?" I showed her my knuckles.

"Jimmy's mother abandoned him with that man. Paints quite a picture, doesn't it?"

"It paints a picture all right," I said grimly. "Of him and a million other kids. Jimmy's not the only kid in the world who had lousy parents."

"That's true, but not everyone handles their problems the same way. As I recall, you had something of a troubled youth yourself, didn't you?"

"Sure," I said. "But I'm not a murder suspect."

"Why do you always do that?" Tanja said as we crawled into the car.

"What are you talking about?"

"The way you shut me out. I understand about your past, Joe. I can help you work through it."

I rolled my eyes. "*Work through it?* What does that even mean? The past happened. You don't work through it, you just move on. What happened *then* is long gone. It's not happening now, and it won't happen again."

"It can help, Joe."

"Yeah? So after we work through my childhood, can we move on to the Kennedy assassination? How about the civil war and the black plague? Can we work through those, too?"

Tanja crossed her arms and fixed her eyes on the road. That meant our conversation was over. I knew her body language well enough to know that. I also knew that once she started giving me the silent treatment, it could last for hours. I had to change the subject fast. We passed the River Road exit and I glanced at the clock on the dash radio.

"So what's the plan?" I said.

She rolled her eyes and turned her head the other way. I tried again. "Jim said his son had been living in Fort Bragg, and that he worked at a junkyard. It shouldn't be too hard to find him, but it'll take two hours to get there."

She fixed me with a glare. "You have somewhere else to be?"

I was trying to think of a tactful way to say I didn't feel like spending the rest of the day trapped in the car with her giving me the silent treatment, but Tanja pulled out her cell phone and dialed Information.

"I'm looking for a junkyard in Fort Bragg," she said. "Yes, that's it. Can you give me an address?" She memorized the information and hung up. When she had finished, she put her phone away and leaned back in the seat with her eyes closed. I took a deep breath. It was going to be a long drive.

Chapter 4

Tanja

Obviously, Joe has some anger issues. Some of it stems from his childhood, some from the things that happened to him while working undercover. I can never be sure which did the most damage, because Joe won't really talk about any of it. He's a good man, but sometimes I feel like there's a time bomb inside of him just waiting to go off.

I know he wouldn't hurt me, or anyone he cares about, but there are many James Pishards out there. I'm afraid that someday Joe will turn violent, and I won't be there to bring him back to his senses. I've spoken to Diekmann about this in private, but I don't know if he's ever mentioned anything to Joe. When I bring the subject up, Joe either makes a joke out of it or pretends he doesn't know what I'm talking about.

I suppose that's normal. It's not uncommon for men to have difficulty sharing deeply personal feelings and experiences. Young boys are taught to be strong and independent. It's part of their nature as well as their culture. I suppose that can be healthy, but when a person has suffered through highly dangerous or difficult situations, he can lose the ability to turn that switch off. These people often perceive feelings as a weakness, and because of their experiences, they won't allow themselves to be weak. Helping a person like that can be a lifelong struggle.

I gave Joe the silent treatment all the way to Fort Bragg. Yes, I did it partly to punish him for his sarcasm, but mostly to let him know what it feels like when someone you love won't communicate with you. By the time we arrived, he was practically begging me to talk to him. Unfortunately, making the connection between my behavior and his own was a leap of logic, and Joe's not the type to dwell on such things. Sometimes my little psychological tricks work on him, sometimes they don't. All I can do is keep trying to get through to him. I have faith that if I'm persistent, it will happen.

It had begun to rain by the time we pulled into Fort Bragg, but for the moment, it was little more than a mist on the windshield. I was half-starved and I felt like my bladder was about to explode. I should have stopped at a gas station, but unfortunately, it was close to five and we were afraid we might miss Jimmy if we took a detour, so we went straight to the junkyard. Just my luck, it turned out that the place was closed on Fridays.

"No," I groaned, staring at the closed sign in the front window.

"I told you we should stop somewhere," Joe said.

"Never mind that now. I see a light inside. I think somebody's here. I'm going to see if they'll let me in."

Joe rolled his eyes as I ducked out of the Suburban and ran for the office. The rain didn't seem like much until I felt it dribbling down the back of my neck. I got a cold shiver and nearly peed in my stretch jeans. I reached the door and started hammering on it.

I could see the bodies of cars piled up behind the slat-ted ten-foot privacy fence, and I could hear a fork-lift moving around back there somewhere. I peered into the window and saw a shadow move somewhere near the back of the building. I hammered on the door again.

At last a woman appeared. When she saw me, she hurried up to the door and made a waving motion.

"We're closed," she shouted through the glass. "Eight a.m., Monday." She was in her late forties with a cheap dye job, and she was puffing on a cigarette. Her orange-red hair fell in tight curls around her shoulders.

"Sorry to bother you," I yelled. "I need to use your bathroom!"

She looked me up and down. I was standing there in the rain, soaking wet and pregnant. I must have looked reasonably pitiful, because she unlocked the door and ushered me inside. "You poor thing, you shouldn't be standing out there in the cold. Look at you, you're soaked! You must be freezing. You're going to catch pneumonia!"

"I'm okay," I said. "I've been driving for hours and I really need a bathroom."

"Of course. It's just down the hall."

I thanked her and hurried in that direction. A few minutes later, I returned to find her working at the front desk. The nameplate on the counter said her name was Marge.

"Feel better?" Marge said as I emerged from the hallway.

"Thanks so much," I said. "That was a close call."

"I understand perfectly," she said. "I've raised three of my own. Pregnancy is fun right up until the shower. Then the party's over. By the end, you just want that thing out."

I laughed. "Does it ever seem like all of nature's cruelest jokes are reserved especially for women? First, it's the menstrual cycles, then the hormones. Then, when we decide to have a baby, our bladders shrink down to the size of a tennis ball and we want to cry every time we see a picture of a puppy or a kitten on the internet. It's absolutely ridiculous."

"I know exactly what you mean. I sent the last one off to college last fall."

"You must be relieved," I said.

"Yes, when I'm not crying. Now that they're all gone, I don't know what to do with myself. I'm just praying for menopause to kick in before I do something stupid. Of course, when that happens, we get a whole new truckload of mood swings and emotional wreckage."

"Maybe you should get a puppy," I said, grinning.

"Sure, one more life to micromanage. That's just what I need. Besides, I'm never home anyway. The poor thing would probably starve to death. Is there anything else I can do for you? I don't mean to rush you off, but I have to finish all this paperwork."

"Actually, I did come here for a reason. I'm trying to track down an employee of yours. Jimmy Pishard."

"Oh, he's not in today. He'll be back on Monday morning."

"I see... I don't suppose you'd mind giving me his address?"

"That's against the rules," she said, looking me up and down. Her eyes lingered on my belly. "Is that baby his?"

I patted my tummy. "Yes. Yes it is."

I walked out of there five minutes later with the address, cell phone number, and a photocopy of his driver's license. I climbed into the suburban and handed the paperwork to Joe.

"Nice work," he said. "How'd you get all this?"

"Social engineering," I said, winking at him.

"Uh-huh. Meaning you lied." He twisted in the seat to face me. "You shamelessly manipulated that woman, didn't you?"

I gave him a mischievous grin. "I'm afraid I have bad news, Joe. The baby isn't yours."

"I see. Won't Jimmy be surprised when he finds out he knocked up a middle-aged woman he never met before."

I made a fist. "What was that you said?"

"Won't Jimmy be-?"

"No, the other part. The *middle-aged part*."

Joe gulped. "I just meant from his perspective, being younger than you and just a-"

"Shut up."

"Okay."

Joe pulled back onto Highway 1 and drove north out of town. A few miles up the road, we turned right and headed down a muddy back road. The rain had stopped, but as the redwoods closed in around us, it became so dark that without the headlights, we'd have been driving blind.

We came to a fork in the road and followed a sign pointing to the right. It was a piece of wood nailed to a tree, and spray painted with Jimmy's address. A minute later, we came to a clearing where a cabin rested next to a creek. Smoke was rolling out of the chimney, and it drifted across the property like a fog. We parked and approached the house.

The owner must have seen us coming, because he opened the door after just one knock. We found ourselves face to face with a gray-bearded man in a buckskin jacket and cowboy hat. He looked us up and down, not saying a word.

"We're looking for Jimmy Pishard," I said.

"Behind the house," the man said with a nod. And with that, he closed the door.

"Friendly," I murmured. "I guess that explains why he lives way out here."

We walked around the cabin and saw a trail leading to a camp trailer a few yards up the hill. "The guy in the house must be Jimmy's landlord," I said.

"Why do you say that? He could be a friend, or somebody Jimmy works with."

"A friend or co-worker would have wanted to know who we were," I said. "This guy either didn't care, or was trying to mind his own business."

"Good point."

As we approached the trailer, I saw a series of extension cords running up from the cabin. There was a light on inside, and I noticed the unmistakable smell of burning propane. "He's home," I said in a low voice.

Joe stepped up to the door and knocked. I was a little nervous as we stood there waiting, listening to the sound of movement inside. Jimmy Pishard didn't know who we were, but that didn't mean he wouldn't come out with guns blazing. He was after all, a murder suspect. I found myself thinking fondly of the Glock in my dresser back home, wishing I'd thought to bring it with me.

That was a strange thought, because in all those years with the FBI, I had never shot anyone. I'd only had to draw my firearm a handful of times, and I had never even come close to pulling the trigger. Until that moment, I had always been opposed to the idea of shooting someone. With Joe standing there next to me, and this tiny little baby growing in my womb, I realized that I would do just about anything to keep them safe.

When the door finally opened, I flinched. Joe gave me a strange look as Jimmy Pishard appeared before us. I recognized him from the pictures, but just barely. He'd changed a lot. The first thing I noticed was that he had put on weight. His hair was even longer than it had been, reaching almost to his waist, and he wore it pulled back in a tail. He was taller, too. Six-three or more. Jimmy had sprouted after high school.

He pushed his wide frame through the doorway, and a cloud of incense followed him out of the trailer. I glanced over his shoulder and saw a book resting on the counter, next to a pot of coffee.

"Can I help you?" he said, looking us up and down.

"I'm Tanja Shepherd. This is my husband Joe. We're private investigators. Do you know why we're here?" His shoulders slumped.

"Do you work for the family, or the cops?"

"Neither," Joe said quickly. I glanced at him and back at Jimmy.

"That's not entirely true," I said. "I won't lie to you, Jimmy. We're trying to find out who killed Becky Sweet. We came to you because we want to hear your side of the story."

He locked gazes with me, and I saw a world of pain and frustration behind his eyes. "Are you sure? Because that's what the cops said last time, right before they arrested me for murder."

"This isn't a trick," I said, trying to sound reassuring. "If you're innocent, Joe and I will prove it. I promise."

He sighed. "All right. I suppose you won't leave me alone until I talk to you anyway. What do you want to know?"

"Did you kill her?"

"Of course not."

"Do you know who did?"

"No."

"Tell us what happened, in your own words."

He stepped around us and gestured down the path.

"There's no room in the trailer, but we can talk over here," he said. He led us a few yards down the trail to a picnic area covered by a canvas canopy. There was a redwood picnic table and an outdoor fireplace made of brick. Joe and I settled down at the table. As he began to speak, Jimmy started building a fire.

"Becky was special to me," he said. "She wasn't like the other pretty girls. They just saw my hair and my clothes. They acted like I was scary or disgusting. Becky wasn't like that."

"What happened?" I said. "Why did the two of you break up?"

"To be honest, I just had too much baggage. I didn't know how to have a relationship and she got tired of me being depressed and moody."

"So she dumped you?" said Joe.

"Things hadn't been going that well. I was tired of my old man beating on me, so I ran away. She tried to talk me out of it, and I yelled at her. She just didn't understand."

"And that was when you killed her?" said Joe.

He snorted. "First, I didn't kill her. Second, we broke up months before she died. By then, I'd been dating another girl for a while. Didn't they tell you that?"

I looked at Joe curiously. "Why didn't they note that in their reports?" I said. "Diekmann's file said the break-up happened right before the murder."

Joe shrugged, and I knew what he was thinking. He didn't believe Jimmy's story.

"The only reason the cops chose me as a suspect was because of my hair," Jimmy said. "The cops in Healdsburg used to harass me every single day. They'd wait for me after school, make jokes about arresting me in front of the other kids. It was a living hell."

I could see Jimmy getting frustrated and angry. Under the bitterness in his voice, I heard pain. I glanced at Joe and wondered if any of it was getting through to him.

"What about the drugs?" he said. "Your file says you admitted to doing drugs."

Jimmy shook his head and laughed. "Is that what they told you?"

"Is it true?" Joe said.

"Aww, man... One of those cops asked me if I'd ever smoked pot. I said *yes* because I wanted to be honest and helpful. I told them I'd tried it once, but I didn't like it and I've never smoked it again. But they didn't write that down, did they?"

He bent down to light the fire, and it quickly blazed up.

"What about the night of the murder?" I said.

"They say Becky was killed down at the dairy farm. That's all I know."

"You weren't near there?"

"I was working, delivering pizzas."

I glanced at Joe. "The notes didn't mention that, either."

"It's not much of an alibi," Joe said. "There's a lot of time between deliveries."

"You think so?" said Jimmy. "Maybe you should try it someday."

41

"What do you mean?" I said.

"You've obviously never worked for a pizza joint. They are always understaffed. I mean *always*. If they need ten workers, they'll hire six. If they need six, they'll schedule three. I lost tips every single day at that job because the manager assigned me so many deliveries that I couldn't possibly get them out on time. If you can do fifteen deliveries an hour and find time to kill someone, you must have a time-traveling DeLorean."

"What about other boyfriends?" I said. "Or somebody at school who had a crush on her? Was there anyone like that?"

"I suppose. Becky was pretty, so she always had guys interested in her. I had to chase off a few while we were dating. She was a cheerleader, so who knows?"

"What do you mean?"

He glanced back and forth between us. "I guess they didn't write that down either," he said. "There were rumors -scandals- happening at the high school. Stories about orgies on the bus, that sort of thing. A couple of cheerleaders got pregnant."

"Did the police investigate it?" I said.

"How should I know? You don't think they told me anything, do you?"

Joe rolled his eyes. "Rumors like that get started all the time. It doesn't mean anything actually happened. I don't see what it has to do with this case."

"It depends," I said. "We'll talk about it later." I handed Jimmy our business card. "If there's anything else you can think of that might help, please call. I promise, we're on your side. We're going to find out who did this."

"It's a little late for that," he said. "Do you have any idea what my life has been like for the last few years? The cops spread my name all over the news. They arrested me *at my job*. They accused me of murder in front of everyone I knew, and put my name in all the papers. I had to come all the way to Fort Bragg just to find somebody who would hire me. Do you really think it matters to me if you're going to find the real killer now? If you really want justice, go after the cops who railroaded me and ruined my life. Otherwise, just leave me alone."

Joe and I walked back to the Suburban in silence. As we turned around in the driveway, I got one last glimpse of the tiny trailer up on the hill and started to cry. I suppose it had more to do with my cascading hormones than anything else, but I still couldn't help it. I felt bad for the kid. I pulled a tissue out of the glove box and dabbed the tears from my eyes.

"What's the matter?" Joe said.

"Jimmy's story just got to me, I suppose."

"He really suckered you, didn't he? So much for those mysterious super-powers to read people that you have."

"I read people just fine."

"So you're saying Jimmy's not the killer? Okay, I'll buy that. But I won't feel sorry for him when all he's done for the last few years is feel sorry for *himself*."

"And what should he have done?" I said.

"He should have gotten over it. Gone to college, found a better job. He didn't have to give up on life."

"How is a kid like that going to pay for college, or find a career?"

"They have programs."

"I see. With the cops harassing him and the whole community treating him like an outcast, you think Jimmy should have gone looking for handouts to get into college... Somehow, I don't think you'd approve of that, either."

"He could have found a better job, at least. Moving to Fort Bragg was the right thing to do. He should have moved even farther away."

"Seriously? It wasn't enough to have the entire community turned against him? He should have moved hundreds of miles away from everything and everyone he'd ever known, all because he just happened to *know someone* who got murdered?"

"You're simplifying things."

"No, Joe. You are simplifying things."

Joe fell silent, and things got quiet long enough for me to wonder if I'd been too hard on him. Thankfully, Joe's cell phone rang before the silence went on too long. He hung up a minute later and tugged on his goatee as he stared at the road ahead of us.

"That was the Sheriff. He wants to see us first thing in the morning."

"Is something wrong?"

"Yeah. James Pishard filed a complaint against us. He says he wants me arrested and charged with assault."

Chapter 5

Joe

Tanja and I walked into the sheriff's department at eight o'clock sharp the next morning. Lucy was manning the front desk, just like she had been every day for the last twenty years. She's a heavyset woman with short black hair, a broad face, and many wrinkles from smiling. She reminds me of a favorite aunt who always brings cookies when she visits.

Lucy looked at me over the rims of her glasses and whispered, "*What did you do, Joe?*"

"Not enough," I said under my breath. Tanja clicked her tongue at me.

"The sheriff is waiting for you in the big conference room," Lucy said. "With lawyers."

"Great."

Tanja and I took the long walk down the hall in silence. I felt like a kid on his way to the principal's office. The sheriff's door was open, and the light streamed out into the darkened hallway. One of Diekmann's cost-cutting measures had been to cut back on the utilities by installing timers on all the lights. It was nice in theory, but with the hallway lights shutting off every five minutes, the overall effect left the place feeling more like a dungeon than an office building. I suppose the mood was appropriate for the occasion.

Diekmann waved us in. I glanced around the room and saw James Pishard sitting at the table with a neck brace, accompanied by two expensive looking lawyer types. The first was a woman with big pearl earrings and a turquoise necklace; the other was a scrawny guy with a bad haircut and thick glasses. In his black suit, the guy looked more like a pallbearer than a lawyer, although I couldn't picture him lifting anything heavier than a briefcase without hurting himself. The sheriff made introductions as he gestured for us to take a seat.

"This is Sandra Stockton, James Pishard's legal counsel, and her assistant Ralph. I believe the two of you already know Mr. Pishard."

I propped my elbows up on the table and cracked my knuckles. "We've met," I said. Tanja glared at me.

"All right. Let's get started."

The lawyer spoke up. "Sheriff, Mr. Pishard has already filled out all the proper forms. Why haven't you arrested this ruffian?"

"Ruffian?" I said. "Who talks like that?"

Tanja elbowed me in the rib cage. Sandra glared at me.

"How would you describe a thug who randomly assaults people he meets?" she said.

"He's the one who sucker-punched me!"

"Quiet," Diekmann said. He turned his attention to Sandra. "I've looked over the paperwork, but there are still a few issues with your claim."

She raised her eyebrows. "Such as? This is an obvious case of assault. I really don't see what might change that."

"Well, there is the question of who struck first," said the sheriff. "I know it sounds like playground politics, but if your client struck Joe first, whatever Joe did afterwards was self-defense."

"It was Pishard," Tanja said. "He started it."

"Semantics," said Sandra. "Besides, you obviously can't consider the testimony of the assailant's *wife*. We'll let the judge decide."

"Alleged assailant," Diekmann corrected her. "Before you start throwing accusations around my department, you'd better get the terminology correct. Which brings me to the second matter: the fact that Joe and Tanja were working for the department at the time of the altercation."

The lawyer glanced at Pishard. He shrugged, but I could tell by the look in her eyes that this new information altered the situation. Her cut and dry assault case was getting deeper in the mud with each passing second.

"And I have witnesses," the sheriff continued, "who say Mr. Pishard laid his hands on Tanja before the fight even began. Two salesmen at the boatyard saw this, and I'm sure the Shepherds will be happy to testify along with them."

Sandra's head snapped around and she glared at Pishard. "Is this true?"

"What difference does it make?"

The sheriff leaned back in his chair. "Perhaps you'd like a closer look at the woman your client assaulted. Whom I hasten to add, was in my employ at the time. Stand up, Tanja. Let them take a look at you."

Tanja beamed as she rose from her chair and turned side to side, proudly displaying her large belly.

"You hit her?" Sandra said to Pishard.

"No, of course not. I just..." he trailed off, realizing he was about to incriminate himself even further.

"He pushed her, and threatened her," I said. "That's why I knocked him on his butt." I glared at

Pishard and added, "Which is where you should have stayed."

"That's it!" Pishard shouted, slamming his fist on the table. "I'm suing all of you. I'm going to own this whole stinking police department!"

Diekmann rolled his eyes. Very patiently, he said, "Ms. Stockton, I recommend you get your client out of my building before I lock him up."

She quickly rose out of her chair and grabbed Pishard by the sleeve. He struggled for a moment and then gave up as he realized that Diekmann was serious. I glared at him the entire time, daring him to make a move. At that point, I didn't care if Diekmann arrested me or not. Our first encounter hadn't taught Pishard the lesson he still needed to learn, and I was aching to teach it to him.

Tanja put a hand on my arm, trying to calm me. Pishard, Sandra Stockton, and Ralph trickled out into the hallway. I made an effort to unclench my fists.

"Put your hackles down," Diekmann said quietly. "Joe, I'd like a word in private. Tanja, help yourself to the donuts in the break room."

"Yes, sir!" she said with a grin.

My shoulders slumped. The sheriff swiveled around in his chair to face me as she closed the door. We were alone, and the look of sheer disappointment on his face made me feel absolutely humiliated.

"Twenty-four hours, Joe. You couldn't even give me twenty-four hours."

"He hit me first," I said. "Besides, he threatened Tanja. What was I supposed to do? I should've broken the guy's neck."

"Maybe, but even so, it's pretty obvious that you're not in control of your emotions."

I laughed. "What are you talking about? I didn't kill him, did I? I ended the confrontation. All I did was hit him a couple times."

"More like eight."

"Huh?"

"There were witnesses inside the building, Joe. And a camera on the lot, too. You beat on that guy pretty hard."

I was stunned. I could clearly remember hitting Pishard after he punched me. I remembered tackling him, slamming him down on the boat... My eyes widened. I couldn't remember anything after that. My next memory was of turning the Suburban around in the parking lot.

"See what I mean?" Diekmann said, as if he'd read my thoughts.

"Bill, it's not like I-"

"It's not what you *did* Joe, it's what you might have done. Trust me, I served in 'Nam. I know what it's like to be walking the streets confused and angry, wondering where you fit in, or if you ever will again. When certain things happen to you, they can change you. Sometimes, you don't even know it. You think everything's fine and then you just suddenly snap."

"I'm not going to go running down the street naked with an assault rifle if that's what you're worried about."

"Perhaps not, but there's only one way to be sure. Do you still have that card?"

I sighed. "At home."

"Good, use it. Don't make me tell you again. If I get another complaint against you, I won't be able to use your services anymore. That's the last thing I want to happen with that baby coming. You need to get your head straight, and do it now."

I nodded.

"Am I understood?" he added.

"Yes. I'll make the call."

"Good. Now get to work."

I found Tanja chatting Lucy up over coffee and donuts at the front desk. I was temped to grab one for myself, but after my talk with the sheriff, I didn't feel much like eating. I just wanted out of there. Tanja saw my look and said goodbye to Lucy. We didn't speak until we were in the car.

"So what did Diekmann want?"

"Nothing."

"Are you sure? You seem upset."

"Of course I am. I can't believe the nerve of Pish- ard, trying to file charges against me. I halfway wish he had, just because I'd love to see him stand in front of a judge with that story."

"Let it go, Joe. I'm sure his lawyer is telling him right now what an idiot he is. Let's focus on our work. We still have a case to solve."

"Fine. Where are we going?"

"The dairy is just across town. Let's go take a look at the crime scene."

"The crime scene? From five years ago?"

"I just want to look around, see if the owner will talk to us. He might have some important information. Based on what we've learned so far, we can't rely on any of the notes in this case. We just have to pretend we're starting from scratch."

"Is that your way of saying Sequoia cops are lousy at their jobs?"

"Not at all. I'm sure they're wonderful at writing speeding tickets."

I glared at her, and she laughed.

The dairy was three miles south of town, on a single lane road that hadn't been paved in at least twenty years. The ditch along the edge of the road had eroded the soil under the pavement, so the asphalt was crumbling and falling away in big chunks. Judging by the rusted old muffler and tire chunks laying on the embankment, the place had caused its share of accidents. Thankfully, we didn't encounter any oncoming traffic.

I turned into a wide gravel lot in front of an old converted house with peeling paint and a sign hanging over the door that said "Office." There were several more buildings scattered across the property, including a large corral with a tin roof. Strangely absent from the dairy were any cows.

The office door was open. When Tanja and I stepped out of the Suburban, a woman dressed in overalls and hip waders came walking out. She had masculine features: broad shoulders, beady close-set eyes, and gray hair that she'd pulled back in a tail. If I'd seen her from behind, I might have mistaken her for a man.

"Can I help you?" the woman said in a husky chain-smoker voice.

"We're looking for the owner," Tanja said.

"You're looking at her. Shelly Smith's the name." She extended a calloused hand. "At least for another twenty-four hours."

"Are you selling the place?" I said.

"Sold it already. As of tomorrow, this is all going to be converted to vineyards."

"I'm sorry to hear that," Tanja said.

51

"Oh, it don't mean much to me. This place always was more work than it was worth. I tried to keep it for my father. He wanted it to stay in the family, but he died fifteen years ago. I've been running the place myself ever since. Up until that girl died here, anyway. After that, the health inspectors shut me down. Gave me a mile of red tape to sort through. I couldn't afford to keep feeding the cattle so I had to sell 'em off. After that, it was just a matter of time."

"What are you going to do now?"

"I'm going to Alaska," the woman said with a grin. "One of them big corporations bought me out, all eighty acres. Five million dollars. *Kapow!*"

"Congrats," I said, laughing. "Sounds like you won the lotto."

Shelly nodded, quite proud of herself. "You better believe it. Not that it wasn't a good deal for them, too. You won't find a more fertile piece of land in a hundred miles. In a few years, they'll be growing grapes the size of basketballs."

"About that girl," Tanja said. "Do you mind if we ask you a few questions?"

"You reporters?"

"No, we're investigators working with the Sequoia Sheriff's Department. We're hoping to find new information on the case."

"Follow me," said Shelly.

She led us across the lot and inside one of the large outbuildings. Upon entering, I instantly recognized it as the scene of the murder. The milk vat where the victim had been found was still sitting there, just a few feet from the doorway. According to Shelly's story, the place hadn't been used since that night. I believed it.

Cobwebs covered all the machinery and a layer of dust covered the floor.

"This is it," she said. "We found her here at four a.m. that morning."

"That's early," I said. "Did you find the body?"

"No, Dennis got here first. We were just getting ready to pump."

"Pump?" said Tanja.

"Yeah, to pump the milk. See, the cows know by habit to walk up to the pumping machines twice a day, first at sunrise, then at sunset. All we have to do is hook up to their udders and turn on the machines."

"And who is Dennis?" Tanja said.

"He used to be my assistant. He'd come out here early in the morning to get the machinery prepped. That's when he found her."

"We don't have anything about him on file," said Tanja. "Do you have any contact information for Dennis?"

"I'll give you what I have. Not sure it's any good, though. I had to let him go years ago. No telling where he is now."

"Anything you have will help."

"One thing you should know about Dennis. He's sort of slow, if you take my meaning. Handicapped, I mean ... he can work just fine and even handle light machinery, but you can't give him more than one job to do at a time, or he'll sure as the world screw everything up."

"We'll keep that in mind," said Tanja. "So what happened when Dennis found the body?"

"Oh, he let out a scream that darn near curdled my blood. I thought he'd chopped off his hand or something. I was still in bed when he came running out of the milk room, waving his hands and hollering about some girl. I followed him back inside and saw what he was talking about, so I sent him to the office to call 911."

"Do you remember anything about the crime scene?" Tanja said. "Any blood, or equipment out of place?"

"Just the wrench the killer used on her. Everything was just the way we left it, except for the body floating in the cream. I always kept this place spotless, not that you'd know it now. That didn't matter to the health inspectors. Once the murder happened, they just wanted to shut me down, that's all."

"Neither of you knew the victim?" I said.

"Nope. We'd never seen her before. She was a pretty girl. They say she was a cheerleader. There was a big write-up about her in the Press Democrat."

"We'll have to check the archives," I said. "Might make it easier to track down her family and friends."

"I've got the paper," Shelly said. "You can have it if you want."

"Are you sure you have it? That was five years ago."

"It's in my file cabinet. Stuck it in there the weekend they shut me down. Ain't looked at it since. Hang on, I'll go get it."

Shelly wandered back in the direction of the office. Tanja and I took a minute to look the place over. We didn't find anything but rust and cobwebs. As we walked out of the building, I noticed that one of the hills across the road looked unusual. From the higher vantage at the end of the parking area, I could see that it had a broad, flat top. When Shelly returned with the paper, I asked her about it.

"Oh, that's not a hill, that's our reservoir," she said. "There was a pond up there originally, but back in the eighteen hundreds, the farmer who owned the place expanded it into a reservoir. He used it for irrigation in the summer. My family never did any farming but we used it for drinking water for the cattle. Dad used to fish trout up there, too, just between you, me, and the fencepost."

"Why?" said Tanja. "Is there something wrong with that?"

"It takes a special permit," I said. "You can't store water without being licensed, and you can't stock fish, or catch them."

"Even on your own property?" she said.

"Especially on your own property," Shelly said with a laugh. "If you're gonna fish without a license, best do it on somebody else's land. Dad didn't care about that, though. The reservoir was legal, but he didn't have a permit for stocking fish. I guess it doesn't matter, now that he's dead and the place is sold."

"I see," said Tanja. "Well thank you very much for your help, Mrs. Smith."

"Sure thing."

"Do you mind if I go up there and take a look?" I said.

"At the reservoir? Suit yourself. Just close the gate on your way out."

"Will do," I assured her. "Enjoy Alaska."

"You bet your booty I will."

We drove a few hundred yards down the public road, to the access point for the reservoir. I jumped out to open the gate. Tanja offered to do it, but I wasn't about to let my pregnant wife go tromping through the mud. After pulling it open, I jumped back in the Suburban and drove up the narrow road to the top of the slope.

Tanja stayed in the car while I got out to look around. I stood on the embankment looking down at the water's edge. I turned my head slowly, taking in the view. The reservoir was surprisingly large; big enough to call a lake. We had parked at the southern end. Trees and bushes sprouted up along the western edge on my left, and north of the lake rose a tall, oak-covered hill. To the east, I could just barely see the roofs of the dairy buildings. Tanja rolled down the window.

"What are you looking for?" she said.

"Becky's car was never found, right?" I said.

"You think her car's in there?"

"I don't know."

I climbed down the slope to the level of the water. I peered into the reservoir, but couldn't see anything in that murky water except the choppy reflection of the sky and my own shaved head. Tanja crawled out of the Suburban and stood at the top of the embankment, looking down on me. She gazed out across the water, shielding her eyes from the sun with one hand.

"Did the file say anything about this reservoir?" I said.

"Not a word."

I started pulling off my boots.

"Joe, what are you doing?"

"Just taking a look."

"Don't tell me you're thinking about going in that water. It's freezing. And disgusting!"

"It's too hazy to see anything up here," I said. "And we don't have the time or money to sweep the whole pond." I pulled off my shirt and dove into the water.

I instantly regretted it. Tanja was right about the water's temperature. It was somewhere around forty-five degrees, but it felt like ice. The second I went under, my entire body went rigid and every instinct I had told me to gasp for breath. I fought the urge, forcing my limbs to move as I paddled towards the surface. I broke through, sucked in a huge gulp of air, and forced myself to dive back under.

Keep moving! was all I could think. It would warm up eventually. It had to.

I dove deeper, paddling cautiously because the sunlight couldn't penetrate more than a few feet of the hazy green water. The last thing I wanted to do was slam my face into a piece of rusty old metal, and cut myself to shreds. I'd be facing a whole slew of shots and antibiotics if I did.

I surfaced again, and treaded water for a few seconds. My lungs were burning, my breath coming in short, abrupt gasps. My skin was beginning to tingle. I told myself it was just my body adapting to the new temperature and not the early stages of hypothermia. My teeth chattered, and I could only stop them by clenching my jaw.

"Do you see anything?" Tanja called out. I shook my head and dove back under.

I spent about ten minutes total in the water. I swam along the banks, where it seemed most likely that the killer might have pushed the car in. When I didn't find anything there, I moved out towards the middle of the lake, thinking perhaps that the vehicle had floated out a ways before sinking.

In the center, I went down three times, each time pushing myself farther, hoping to find the car, or at least to find the bottom. I didn't find either one, but I did manage to make my ears pop so painfully that I cried out. When I finally gave up and returned to shore, I was shaking uncontrollably, and my skin had taken on an unhealthy bluish pallor.

"What were you thinking?" Tanja said as I donned my dry shirt. I climbed into the passenger seat, turned on the heat, and pushed my hands and feet pushed up to the heater vents.

"H-h-had to l-l-look," I stammered.

"Had to give yourself hypothermia is more like it. What's the matter with you, anyway? You're not twelve anymore, Joe. You could have given yourself a heart attack."

"N-nah," was all I could manage.

Tanja took over driving duties, even though she hated driving when she was pregnant. She guided the Suburban down the slope very cautiously, because she couldn't see the edges of the road. At the bottom, I hopped out to close the gate. I grimaced as the sharp gravel on the road bit into my bare feet. It was then, as I latched the gate and limped back to the car, that I realized she was right. I *was* an idiot. Not that I was going to tell her that.

We were halfway home by the time my fingers were warm enough to lace my boots back up. Tanja was about to turn down our street when I stopped her.

"Wait," I said. "Let's pay Grandma a visit."

"Now?" she said, mystified.

"Yeah. I just thought of something."

"What are you talking about?"

"I'll show you when we get there."

Tanja rolled her eyes, but followed my instructtions. She knows it's a waste of time arguing with me when I get in these moods. I tend to spring things on her all the time. That's because things never work out when I plan. Sometimes, it seems like there's some universal force out there listening to everything I say, just waiting to screw up my plans as soon as I announce them.

I never plan camping trips ahead of time, for example. If I talk about it, something will go wrong. It always does. One of us will be called into work, the weather will turn stormy, or something else will go wrong. So, instead of planning ahead, I wait until the night before. I tell her we're leaving early the next day. Tanja hates it of course, but she has learned to trust my instincts. She's seen the stupid things that happen when I *don't* act spontaneously.

When we pulled off the road leading to my grandmother's property in Alexander Valley, I had two things in mind. The first was to find out if she'd kept grandpa's old aluminum fishing boat. If she had, I wanted to take it back to the reservoir and use the fish finder to search for underwater objects. That was the only way to be sure if that car was on the bottom of the lake or not. The second was to tell her that I'd had a talk with Sheriff Diekmann and that she didn't need to worry about me. I'd be just fine.

As we pulled into the drive, I saw Diekmann's truck parked in front of the house and I forgot everything else. My mind instantly assumed the worst. Grandma had fallen down... or, God forbid, had a heart attack...

"Oh, no," Tanja said. "Joe, I hope Grandma's okay."

I didn't say anything. I had my seatbelt off and the door open before she could even stop the car. I jumped out, ran to the front door and burst in without knocking. Standing in the entryway next to the living room, I shouted, "Grandma! Are you okay?"

"Just a minute," she called from upstairs. "I'm getting dressed. I'll be right down!"

I frowned, wondering what the heck Grandma was doing without her clothes on at four o'clock in the afternoon. Then I remembered Diekmann's truck parked outside.

Chapter 6

Joe

Half an hour later, I was on the redwood deck out back, flipping burgers on the barbecue and staring out across the vineyards. I was sipping a beer. It wasn't my first and it wouldn't be my last. Diekmann wasn't drinking; he was just staring guiltily at the mountain range to the north. Tanja watched me with a quiet, discomforting gaze while Grandma was somewhere inside, cutting tomatoes and sautéing mushrooms for the burgers.

That was how it had been for an hour. Quiet, uncomfortable, the only words spoken done so in haste as if every syllable might potentially set off a bomb. They were all walking on eggshells, and it was because of me. I knew it, but what was I supposed to say? Sure, Grandpa had been dead for ten years. It was only natural for Grandma to crave companionship... but Sheriff Diekmann?

And this wasn't a game of bridge or teatime with her lady friends. This was *sex*. My stomach churned. She was seventy for God's sake. Seventy-year-old grandmas don't have sex. They. Just. Don't. And no one would ever convince me otherwise.

"How are the burgers, Joe?" Grandma said through the kitchen window.

"A few more minutes."

After another long silence, I couldn't take it anymore. I stared at Diekmann.

"We visited with Shelly Smith this afternoon," I said.

"Smith?" he said, gazing into the distance. It took a few seconds for him to remember. "The dairy farm owner? Don't tell me she was any help."

"Not really. I would like to get a closer look at that reservoir, though."

"What reservoir?"

I told him briefly about my exploration of the frigid lake. Tanja added in her bit about me acting like an idiot and diving right in, which Diekmann found amusing but managed not to laugh.

"I think sonar might do the trick," I said. "I'd like to go back there tonight."

"I'm sure my men would have considered that at the time."

"There's nothing about it in the file."

He considered that. "They wouldn't have overlooked something so obvious. More likely, they checked the area for tracks and didn't find any. Or, the water was so low at the time that it wasn't even suspect."

"That would make sense," said Tanja, "but it would have been nice for them to note that in their reports. Unfortunately, we can only guess now as to what they did or did not do."

Diekmann looked askance at me. "I think I'm being lectured."

"Welcome to my world," I said. Tanja threw her beer cap at me. I ducked, and it went sailing out across the lawn.

"I suppose it wouldn't hurt," said Diekmann. "But why tonight? What's the rush? Becky's been dead five years, and if the car has been in that pond all this time, it's not going anywhere."

"Shelly just sold the farm. The new owner is taking possession tomorrow. She gave us permission to investigate the lake, so I want to do it tonight, while she still owns it. We might not get another chance to check it out."

"It'll probably be a lot of work for nothing."

"Maybe, but I'd rather know it was for nothing than have it nagging at me because I never looked into it."

"All right, I'll go with you."

I glanced at Tanja and saw her smiling. I could see her gears turning. She thought this was some sort of male bonding thing. Bonding over the fact that Diekmann and my grandma were... *ugh.* Not bloody likely.

"You sure?" I said. "It'll be cold and dark. Wouldn't want you to catch pneumonia."

"Very funny," said Diekmann. "I may be old, but I'm not that fragile. I'll give you a hand pulling that boat out of the barn after dinner. You're not turning down an official escort by the sheriff are you?"

"I suppose not."

"Good," Tanja said with a radiant smile. "It's settled. You two do that, and I'll stay here with Grandma to catch up on the gossip."

I bet you will, I thought with a grimace.

It turned out that Grandma had saved Grandpa's boat all those years, but what she didn't tell us was that Grandpa had stored it in the rafters of the barn. Not only that, but the rope and pulley system he'd used to get it up there had been rusting and rotting for ten years. Getting the thing safely to the floor without destroying the boat or hurting ourselves was like performing brain surgery with a machete.

It took an hour and a few minor bruises to get the boat down, and another to get it loaded safely on top of the suburban. The only good luck we had was that the sonar was still mounted inside, and after we'd changed the batteries, it appeared to be working just fine.

Diekmann and I finally got to the reservoir around midnight. By the time we had parked, a storm had begun to move in and we could see flashes of lightning over the mountains towards the coast. That was when my hip decided to gimp up on me. Unfortunately, I hadn't brought my cane because I had been doing so well for the last few days. My swim in the icy water earlier that day must have set it off, because suddenly I was walking like a pirate with a peg leg.

That meant the two of us -Diekmann, a sixty-eight year old man well beyond the prime of his life, and me, hobbled by my injury- had to unload the boat and get it to the water in the dark. We must have made quite a sight as the two of us worked frantically to get the boat unloaded and launched before the rain came. It might have been funny if it wasn't so frustrating.

By the light of the headlights, we somehow managed to get the boat down to the shore. After that, I had to shut them off for fear of the battery going dead. I had to find my way back down the embankment in the dark, with my bad hip threatening to give out on me any second. Diekmann waited patiently at the shoreline, holding the boat halfway on dry land. As I reached him, the wind began to blow and I knew it wouldn't be long before the rain started.

I steadied the old aluminum hull while Diekmann climbed in. I jumped in after him, and grabbed the oars. I got three pulls away from shore before it began to rain.

"Christ almighty," Diekmann said as he fired up the sonar. "I don't know what you did Joe, but you've got some bad karma."

"Maybe it's not me," I grumbled. My frustration gave me strength I didn't know I had. With a few more strokes, we were out in the middle of the lake. I started to turn the rowboat, moving it in a slow circle around the reservoir as Diekmann watched the sonar display.

"I don't blame you," Diekmann said. "In your shoes, I'd be upset, too. But I think you should know you're behaving like a spoiled brat."

I pulled the oars out of the water and leaned forward, staring at him. "Come again? Last time I checked, you were the one taking advantage of your friendship with my Grandma to get laid."

For a second there, it looked like Diekmann might reach across the boat and smack me. Instead, he turned his attention back to the sonar. "I understand why you said that. You're angry. I want you to understand that it was your grandmother who reached out to me, not the other way around. I never would have initiated this, Joe. Your grandfather was too good a friend. I wouldn't do that to his memory. Your grandmother is lonely though, and she has a right to move on. Both of us do, whether you want us to or not. Just because you don't understand it, doesn't mean she should have to be alone the rest of her life."

I grimaced, imagining the two of them in each other's arms. "It's her decision," I grumbled. "As long as she doesn't get hurt."

"Oh, come on, Joe. Quit talking to me like a stranger. I've known you since you were running around the farm in diapers. You know that I'd never do anything to hurt you or your grandmother. You know me better than that. Or, at least I thought you did."

I turned guiltily away, staring at the shore. "Fine. Can we talk about something else?"

He snorted and shook his head. "We've been around the lake twice and I haven't seen anything yet. Why don't you take her over by that clump of bushes? It looks like there may have been a dock over there once."

I turned the boat and headed in that direction. At first, I couldn't make out anything on the shore except for the shadowy silhouette of shrubs and small trees. As we got closer, the moon came out from behind a cloud and I saw two posts rising up out of the water, right at the water's edge.

"You're right!" I said. "You've got good eyes, for an old fart."

"Uh-huh. And I can walk in a straight line, too. Even at my age." He snorted at his own cleverness, poking fun at my gimp leg. I ignored him. I pulled a hard reverse stroke on the right oar, bringing it about so that we could glide in towards the dock without getting caught under the bushes.

"Wait!" Diekmann said. "Hold it right here!"

I pushed back on the oars, trying to slow our movement. Diekmann moved to the side of the bench, and turned the sonar so I could see the screen. "Right there," he said, pointing at a reddish blob outlined in yellow. "It's right under the bow."

"Are you sure?"

"It's the right size. I don't know what else would be down there the size of a Chevy. Look at the shape." I leaned closer, holding the oars up out of the water.

"It does seem rectangular," I said. "Solid, too. Could just be what's left of the old dock."

"Judging from the condition of those old posts, and the growth of those bushes, I'd say that dock has been underwater a long time. I seriously doubt it would be down there in one piece."

I stared at the blob of color, wondering if we'd really found it. It almost seemed too easy. That is, aside from the cold, the rain, and my throbbing leg. On second thought, it wasn't that easy at all. And we still weren't sure we'd found it.

"Could be anything," I grumbled. "An old boat, watering tank, maybe even a pump of some kind."

"We won't know until we get down there."

"I'm not diving down there," I said.

"No need. Tomorrow morning, I'll find out who the new owner is and ask permission to bring a dive team."

"What if he says no?"

"I'll call the judge and get a warrant. I can do that, you know."

I leaned over the edge of the boat, pushing the oar straight down into the water as far as I could reach. The handle disappeared. I continued, pressing my arm into the waves all the way past my elbow. The cold water lapped at the hull as I stretched my arm ever deeper into the chilly depths.

I couldn't help wondering what sort of creatures might live in there. Nothing dangerous, I told myself. Then again, even if there wasn't anything dangerous in there, the whole reason I was there was to find a dead girl's car. That was creepy enough in itself.

I was in almost up to the shoulder, barely hanging onto the end of the handle, when I felt the oar hit a smooth hard surface. Diekmann heard the sound and raised his eyebrows.

"That sounded like metal," he said.

"Maybe."

A current under the water twisted the oar in my fingertips, and it slid out of my grip. It came up floating next to us. I lunged for it and caught it just before it drifted out of reach. The boat rocked precariously, and Diekmann grabbed at the gunwales, steadying himself.

"Dammit, boy!" he said. "I'm too old for a midnight dunking."

"Don't kid yourself; this lake's no colder than the rain."

"All the same, I think I'll stay up here, if you don't mind."

I ignored him. I pushed the oar down into the water again, feeling around, searching the depths for that mysterious surface. Once again, I found a smooth, hard plane about twelve feet below the waves. When the oar made contact, I moved it back and forth to verify that the object was indeed flat, and as large as it seemed. It was.

It could only have been the roof of Becky's car. I couldn't think of anything else that size or shape that might be down there. I lifted the oar out of the water. I stared at Diekmann, ignoring the rain beating down on my head and the cold water soaking up my sleeve and around my collar.

"We found it." I said, hardly believing my own words.

Diekmann smiled. "Congratulations. Now let's get out of here before we get hypothermia or worse yet, capsize this tug and end up down there with it. I'll call in a dive team in the morning."

"What about the sale?" I said. "Are we going to need a warrant?"

"Probably."

I rowed us back to shore, and Diekmann helped me pull the rowboat up onto the embankment. We didn't bother trying to reload it onto the Suburban. We could do that in the morning. We'd both had our fill of the rain for one night, and I was on the verge of hypothermia for the second time in a single day. We climbed into the Suburban, cranked up the heater, and headed for home.

The ladies had already gone to bed when the sheriff and I got back to the farm. Not surprising, since it was almost three a.m. Diekmann took pity on me and went home to sleep in *his own* bed. I had a feeling he wanted to go shower and get some dry clothes anyway.

I found Tanja fast asleep in the guest room upstairs. I stripped my wet clothes off and left them hanging in the bathroom. I was about to crawl into bed with her, when I noticed a slip of paper on the floor. It appeared to have fallen out of her jeans, which she had hung over the back of a chair by the window. Thinking it might be important, I scooped it up. I was just going to toss it on the chair, but something about it caught my attention. It didn't appear like just *any* piece of paper. It had the look and feel of a check, folded in half.

Without a second thought, I opened it up. To my surprise, I found out that was exactly what it was. A check for twenty-five hundred dollars, signed by my grandmother and made out to Tanja and me. Instantly, my head was swimming. I tried to summon up some reason that my grandmother would be giving us money. To start a trust fund for the baby, or perhaps she wanted to buy a share of our business. I came up with half a dozen hair-brained ideas, trying to consider anything but the obvious, which was that Tanja had borrowed money to pay our bills.

That idea made me sick to my stomach. It wasn't just that she'd done it behind my back. That was bad enough. There was also the fact that she'd been hiding money problems from me. I had known our savings was nearly tapped out for a while, but for some reason it never occurred to me that it might be *gone*. I couldn't accept that. Not this close; not when we finally had a case to work on and a chance to put our business on the map. I couldn't accept the idea that we might be losing it all, so close to breaking free.

I found myself lying awake in bed for hours, staring up at the ceiling, trying to think about something else. It wasn't easy. Sooner or later, my mind always came back around to that check, and every time I started to think about it, I started to get angry. I wanted to blame Tanja at first. After that, the two of them for being so secretive about it. In the end, it all came around to me.

I always let Tanja handle the bills. I'm no good with numbers. Doing all those calculations is incredibly frustrating for me, so I hand that part of our responsibilities over to my wife. It seems fair enough. After all, she's not the one crawling under the car on a rainy Saturday morning to change the oil, right? A relationship is about sharing responsibilities.

No matter how I argued it out in my head, in the end I knew it was at least as much my fault as hers. I was the one who'd bought the house. Heck, I was the one who'd run out and traded in the old Jeep for a Suburban the same weekend I found out Tanja was pregnant. At the time, it had seemed like a good idea. The Chevy was a year-old loaner car, very gently used with low mileage and all the options. I got it for a steal. But even though the payments were low, they were still there, sucking the money out of our savings month after month.

Of course, I had expected to have a better income eventually. Who doesn't? The problem was that I hadn't counted on the depth of the economic recession, or the devastating effect it would have on the California economy. I had no idea at the time how long it would be before we found work. I certainly never would have guessed that we'd end up starting our own business.

All of that was my fault, too. I was the one who'd insisted Tanja leave the FBI to find something safer, even though I was still unemployed at the time. I'd spent money as if I *had* it, which is about the dumbest thing a person can do, whether he actually has it or not. I was so angry and frustrated with myself that I wanted to think about anything else, just so I could get to sleep. This brought me back around to Diekmann and Grandma, and left me wrestling with a completely different set of emotions.

Ten years. It had been ten long years since Grandpa died, and I had no right feeling as if Grandma should hide herself away from the world and wait for death. Logically speaking, I knew that. But it was this feeling deep inside that was bothering me. The feeling that something might happen to her the way it had to my parents.

That was silly, of course. I knew my parents had chosen to abandon me, and that Grandma would never do that, but I still had some bizarre subconscious fear about the whole thing. I felt like Grandma moving on with her life would mean the end of *our* relationship. It was a stupid, childish thing, but I was worried that with a new romance in her life, Grandma wouldn't be there for me anymore. That I'd be alone, just like I had been as a child.

I just needed to suck it up. Diekmann was a good man. He'd been like an uncle to me for as long as I could remember. The problem was that every time I thought of him with Grandma, I also thought of him laughing and talking with Grandpa, because that was how it had always been. Only it wasn't that way anymore. Grandpa was gone, and now two lonely, aging people had found a chance to be happy together. I had no right to put myself into the middle of it.

This of course left me feeling stupid and angry all over again.

At some point, I finally drifted off to sleep. Tanja woke me at seven thirty, and it seemed like I'd been out for about an hour. I rolled over to go back to sleep, but Tanja said: "The Sheriff called. He said a diving crew will meet us in an hour." My eyes snapped open.

"I'll get dressed!"

It didn't matter how tired I was, there was no way I was going to miss the removal of that car. I threw on my damp clothes and shoveled down a plate of breakfast. I apologized to Tanja and Grandma for coming in so late the night before, because I didn't have the courage to apologize for what I should have. At that point, neither one of them even knew I'd seen the check. I decided that conversation was best saved for later, when we had more time.

Within the hour, Tanja and I were back at the reservoir. Diekmann was already there with a handful of

72

deputies and a tow truck. The dive team had just finished dragging a cable down to the car. I grabbed my cane, which we had picked up from home on the way through town, and limped over to see him with Tanja at my side.

"I see the new owner didn't give you any trouble," I said as we greeted him.

"No. He's not even here. His agent contacted him back in New York to get permission for the search."

"New York?" said Tanja.

"Half the land around here is owned by people from other states," Diekmann explained. "Having a vineyard in Sequoia is like having a beach house in Malibu, or a ranch in Montana. It's a trinket; a status symbol."

"But this isn't a vineyard," she said.

"Not yet," said Diekmann. "But the permits are already on file. By the end of the year, this'll be a ten thousand case winery. The vines will be in the ground before spring. They might even get their first harvest within two years."

As we spoke, a news van drove up the hill and parked at the southern end of the lake. Two workers began setting up equipment outside the van while a reporter hurried over in our direction, followed closely by a cameraman. The reporter was a young blonde woman, very attractive and very overdressed for the tromp along the muddy banks of a reservoir. She smiled as she joined us.

"Hello, sheriff. Nice to see you again."

"Morning, Mary. It didn't take you long to get out here."

"No thanks to you. We had to hear about it on the scanner. Do you mind if we do an interview?"

"Let's wait and see how it goes," Diekmann said. "Right now, we're not even sure if this is the right car... Mary, meet Joe and Tanja Shepherd. They're the investigators who cracked the case."

Mary shook hands with us. "Do you work for the sheriff's department?"

Tanja explained the situation, and told her that we were private detectives.

"You're a married couple, and you're private investigators?" she said. "Fascinating! Do you think we could arrange a televised interview for one of our programs? I do a weekly spotlight on local businesses. It might give you some great publicity."

Tanja glanced at me, and I shrugged. I'm no fan of being in the limelight, but I was willing to do just about anything to give our business a jumpstart. Anything short of standing on the corner, dancing with a sign. There are some things a man just won't do. Not many things, but some.

"Sure, why not?" Tanja said.

"Great, here's my card."

Mary turned her attention back to Diekmann. "Sheriff, can I do a live spot right here, while they pull the car out?"

"It's a free country. But I'll warn you; this is going to be a muddy mess in a few minutes."

"I'll take my chances," she said with a grin.

We stood back a few yards. Mary positioned herself between the lake and the camera, and began to talk. "Hi, I'm Mary Sinclair of Channel 7 News..."

The tow truck driver activated the controls on the back of his truck and flipped a switch. There was a whining sound as the winch drum began to roll. The

74

steel cable went taught and the water along the shore began churning with bubbles.

Mary finished her introduction and stood back, allowing the cameraman a clear shot as the bumper of the car came into view. Within a few seconds, the tail end of the car appeared. I knew at first sight that it was our '69 Camaro.

"That's it," I said, glancing at Diekmann. He nodded quietly.

Slowly but surely, the windows crested the waterline, and a minute later the hood appeared. The once bright red Camaro was now green with moss, and rusted halfway to nothing. A flood of water came pouring out of the fenders and rocker panels as the car slowly moved up the embankment. The windows were a haze of mud and slime, and plants were growing on the roof and hood. The tires refused to roll, but the power of the tow truck's winch would not be denied.

The truck driver disarmed the winch, allowing the car to rest as the water gushed out. Mary and the cameraman went to high ground. I waited for the tsunami to subside and then hurried down to the vehicle, carefully placing my weight on my cane as I slogged through the mud.

I pulled the passenger door open and a wave of muddy water spilled out over my pant legs. I peered inside, doubtful that any evidence would have survived all those years underwater. I pulled my head out and gave the sheriff a dark look.

"You'd better come see this," I said.

"What is it?"

"Sheriff, there's another body in here."

Chapter 7

Tanja

Men. Who do they think they are? They don't have to deal with hormones or periods, they can't even imagine what it's like to carry a baby inside them for nine months. They rarely cook, clean, or do any laundry or really anything useful at all. Except for changing the oil. They sure let us hear about that. Then they hand *us* the checkbook and tell *us* to make it all work. As if the ability to use a calculator somehow turns a woman into a financial wizard. Like we should be able to solve all of the world's financial problems by waving a magic wand.

When it doesn't work out, whose fault is it? You guessed it: It's the woman's fault! But I'm getting ahead of myself...

When I got up that morning, I had no idea that Joe had seen the check from his grandmother. I hadn't been hiding it from him. In fact, I'd planned to tell him about it as soon as we got home, but things kind of snowballed. Grandma asked me to help her make some biscuits and gravy (Joe's favorite), which I did. As soon as that was done, Sheriff Diekmann called and told us all about their adventure at the reservoir. I put him on speaker so Grandma could listen. By the time the conversation was over, we were both cheering over the good news. The case was closed, or at least close to it.

By then, I'd completely forgotten about the check. My mind was on other things. I got Joe out of bed, we had a quick breakfast, and we headed back to the reservoir. The rest, as you know, is history. We found Becky's car, but that's not all we found. The second body inside the car was male. It was impossible to determine much more than that right away.

The coroner -a balding man in his forties with thick glasses, named Henry Halverson- made an examination of the victim and the vehicle's interior. He didn't bother looking for fingerprints or blood splotches, because five years underwater would have washed away or corroded any evidence of that nature. Instead, he focused on trying to find hairs and fibers, or other evidence that may have survived the years of submersion.

He carefully analyzed and documented various articles of clothing, jewelry, and whatever else he found on the corpse. The condition of the body made the task difficult; it was little more than a skeleton draped in tattered shreds of cloth. One thing he noticed right away was that one of the ribs had been broken.

"This was most likely a fresh injury," Henry said. "Most people don't go walking around with a broken rib."

"There must have been a struggle," Joe said.

"Possibly, or it could have happened when the vehicle crashed off the dock. I suspect something else, though." He held up the broken piece of rib, and pointed to the break at the end. "Note the shape of the fracture, and the superior positioning? This indentation and splintering indicates that something struck the bone sharply. This was not a large, blunt object."

"A knife?" said Joe.

"Possibly. I need to examine the bone under a microscope. The skeleton has been degrading in the water for years, so the bone is smoother than it used to be. I might be able to tell more after my examination."

Henry went back to work with the deputies. They began by unbolting the seat, then cautiously removing the seat belt and the center console. After working very carefully for the better part of an hour, they finally lifted the entire bucket seat out of the car with the remains intact, and placed it all on a tarp beside the vehicle. As they moved the body, something fell through the seat and hit the floorboards with a metallic *ping*. A few seconds later, Henry used his flashlight to investigate the noise. He retrieved a small object, which he held up in his tweezers for us to examine. It was a mushroomed bullet.

"He was shot?" said Diekmann.

"That would explain the broken rib," Henry said. "I can't say it's the cause of death, but I'll take some measurements at the lab and see if I can put together a scenario."

Diekmann crossed his arms. "Speculate," he said.

Henry pinched his chin. "Okay... the bullet struck the rib approximately two inches from the sternum. Based on the location, the wound was very close to the heart, if not a direct hit. I believe it was a jacketed slug, meaning it probably would have passed through the body entirely if it hadn't struck the rib. However, the bullet struck the upper edge of the rib, not the center, and therefore probably still had velocity after impact."

"Meaning?"

"Meaning that after hitting the rib, the bullet mushroomed out like a hollow point and continued moving through soft tissue. Even if the bullet missed

78

the heart, the victim probably suffered massive hemorrhaging and catastrophic organ damage. If he wasn't killed immediately, I doubt he would have survived more than a few minutes. That's a quick and dirty assessment, of course. I may reach a different conclusion back at the morgue."

"I understand. Thanks, Henry."

"One more thing: He wasn't shot it in the car. The body was moved here later."

"Are you sure?"

"Almost one hundred percent. Notice the trajectory of the wound. Someone would have had to hold the weapon directly in front of him."

"Not easy in a car this size," I said.

"Exactly."

Henry stored the bullet in an evidence bag and returned to examine the body and the car's interior for more clues. The sheriff turned to face Joe and me.

"Okay, detectives. Now it's your turn to speculate."

We glanced at each other. "Well, they were obviously killed together," Joe said. "The question is how this victim ended up in the lake while Becky ended up in the dairy."

"The killer pushed the car into the lake to hide it," I said. "Becky should have been in there, too. I think this John Doe was killed first, and Becky ran down the hill to the dairy, trying to get away. That's the only thing that makes sense."

"Agreed," said Joe. "The killer chased after Becky and caught her in the dairy, but he was interrupted before he could finish the job. So he dumped her in the vat. Depending on the timing of everything, he may have come back up here afterwards to hide the car."

"Assuming the altercation started here, and also assuming that there was just one killer."

Diekmann considered that, and nodded his head. "Let's go with your theory for now. Until we have some lab results, I can't think of any better explanation for what happened here. I want you two to find out how Becky and the second victim were connected. We'll go from there."

"So we're still on the case?" Joe said.

"Of course you are." Diekmann pulled off his baseball cap and ran a hand through his mussed-up hair. "I want you two to finish this. You've already accomplished more in one day than my department has in the last five years. This second body may be the break that blows this case wide open. I'd hate for someone else to get credit for that. Take what you've got and run with it."

Until that point, I'd had a growing concern that Diekmann might reopen the case and take it away from us, or even call in the FBI With the discovery of the second body, he had every right to do that, and all of our work would have been for nothing. Not knowing Diekmann as well as Joe, I had no idea how he might react to the situation.

My thoughts immediately turned to the foreclosure notice in the kitchen drawer back home. I still hadn't found a way to tell Joe about it. I'd been telling myself that if we could just close this case, I might not have to. In my mind, I had built up this fantasy where everything just fell into place for us. Unfortunately, the real world rarely works out the way it does in day-dreams. When Diekmann said we were still on the case, I sighed with relief.

"You okay?" the sheriff said.

"Of course," I said, forcing a smile. "Just thinking about where to go from here."

At that moment, Henry interrupted us with a shout. "I think we have an I.D., Sheriff!" He hurried over to us, holding up a wallet. Diekmann accepted it, and carefully unfolded it. The leather was intact, but immediately began to tear.

"Looks like he was a reporter," he said, displaying a laminated press badge for the *Chronicle*. The letters were blurred and hard to read. If they had been any smaller, we never would have known what that card said. Diekmann turned the wallet sideways and pulled out a driver's license. The plastic was brittle and the edge chipped the moment he touched it. Enough ink remained that he could just barely make out the name:

"Randall Rosen," Diekmann said. "Looks like a San Francisco address. We might be able to pull more off the magnetic strip, if it's still any good." He handed the card off to one of the deputies. "If nothing else, he should be on file at the Chronicle."

At that moment, one of the deputies finally managed to get the trunk open. He stood back with a perplexed look on his face and said, "Sheriff, take a look at this."

We joined him at the back of the car and stared into the trunk. I was half-afraid it might be another body. It wasn't. It was a well-rusted pickaxe and a shovel. The handles of both were almost completely rotten. I frowned.

"Why would a seventeen year old girl have a pickaxe and shovel in her trunk?"

"Maybe she moonlighted as a gold miner," said Joe.

"Very funny. Does this mean you're going to pursue that lifelong dream as a standup comedian?"

"I have a theory," he said. "Becky killed John Doe and brought him up here to bury him."

"Joe, if Becky killed John Doe, then who killed Becky?"

"The other miner," Joe said with a mischievous grin. "She jumped his claim!"

I took a deep breath. "Is it time to talk to a doctor about your A.D.D. problem?"

He winked at me.

"We'll keep these for evidence, just in case," said the sheriff. "Henry, do you need anything else?"

"No, sheriff, you can take the car now."

"Where is the storage warehouse?" I said. "We might need this car later."

"We don't have a warehouse," Diekmann said. "It's going to the impound yard."

"But the weather!" I said. "What if it rains, or freezes? Evidence could be destroyed."

"It has been underwater for five years," Diekmann said. "Whatever was going to happen to it already has."

"This isn't the FBI," Joe reminded me. "The sheriff can't afford to rent a warehouse every time we take a car into evidence." He saw my glare and added, "But maybe we could cover it with a tarp?"

"Of course," the sheriff said quickly. "Absolutely. We wouldn't want any evidence getting... washed off." He waved at the tow truck driver. "Okay, take her out of here!" He turned to face us.

"I'll be heading back to the department. I have a stack of forms the size of Mount Shasta on my desk. I'll be there all afternoon if you need me."

"We'll call you when we have another break in the case," Joe said.

I just smiled. I wished I shared Joe's confidence. I felt like the discovery of that car was just dumb luck. That wasn't true, though. The real reason was Joe's tenacity. The man is as stubborn as a mule. He had proven that not just by swimming around in that freezing cold reservoir, but by coming back a second time, in the rain, late at night. Not that I really needed any proof of Joe's dogged nature. It takes a certain kind of person to make a living doing undercover work. If Joe had been a person to give up easily, he never would have succeeded.

He also would have been a lot easier to live with.

Joe and I went home after that. He called the San Francisco Chronicle and explained our situation to a Human Resources manager.

"We have an appointment in the morning," he said as he hung up. "In the meanwhile, why don't we track down Becky's mom?"

"That's just what I was thinking," I said. "I'd like to know what was going on in Becky's life at the time of her death. Her mother might know our second victim, too. If we can establish a relationship between Becky and this reporter, we can kill two birds with one stone."

Diekmann's file showed Becky Sweet's address on Fitch Mountain Road in the nearby town of Healdsburg. Her mother's name was Kendra, and a quick internet search confirmed that she still lived there. After I had a quick restroom break, we headed north.

I suppose the brief drive may have been a good time to bring up the foreclosure notice, but for some reason, I didn't. I suppose I was making excuses. The last thing I wanted was to get in another fight with Joe. I still hadn't told him about the check from Grandma either, and it was too complicated to explain on the short drive. Better saved for later, when we had more time...

"That's Fitch Mountain," Joe said as we pulled off the highway. He nodded towards a steep, round-domed peak in the distance. "Kendra Sweet's house is behind that mountain."

I took off my sunglasses and stared. "It looks like a volcano."

"About three million years ago. It's extinct."

"Are you sure?"

Joe smiled. "You never know."

As we drove through Healdsburg, Joe explained that when he was young, the area had been a small farming community. Over the years, as the wine industry grew, big corporations and wealthy investors bought up much of the land to plant vineyards. It wasn't long before Healdsburg became a popular tourist destination. Inevitably, prices skyrocketed, forcing locals to move out.

"Now the place is overcrowded, overpriced, and full of antique-hunting yuppies," he said.

"Aren't we yuppies?"

"Not on the money we make."

"Good point."

As we headed towards Fitch Mountain, the street became narrow and winding. The road began to climb, and the redwoods closed in around us. Through the trees, I caught glimpses of the Russian River twisting through the valley to the north.

I quickly realized that because of the steep terrain, most of the houses on Fitch Mountain had been built on stilts. There were very few parking areas. I saw narrow pullouts that ran lengthwise along the road, and parking stalls on stilts alongside the cottages. I imagined parking our Suburban on one of them, with its three tons of weight resting on those narrow posts, and a shiver crawled up my spine.

"How can this be safe?" I mumbled.

Joe pulled into one of the pullouts along the street. Because the pullout was so small, he parked with the nose of the Suburban stretching out across the broken pavement. I didn't say anything because Joe's parking job was at least as good as the others in the vicinity.

Kendra Sweet's address was just across the street. As we crossed the road, I had to stop and stare at the bizarre structures built up and down the mountainside. The scene looked like the cover of a fantasy novel.

"How can people live in houses built on stilts like this?" I said. "One good earthquake and they'll all be in the river."

"If the mountain doesn't come down on top of them first."

"The mountain! You mean the volcano?"

"Welcome to NorCal," Joe said, laughing. "Good news, it looks like she's home."

We stepped onto a small redwood porch in front of the house, and Joe knocked on the door. He stood back, leaning slightly on his cane. There was a sign hanging from the roof that read: *"Massage & Aromatherapy"*

We heard movement inside, and a woman in her fifties answered the door. The smell of patchouli and incense washed over us. She had gray hair and wore a dress made of hemp. She wore no makeup, but on her fingers were a dozen rings, mostly silver, and she wore several necklaces and thongs with pendants made of crystals, pentacles, and other pagan symbols. She was also barefoot.

"Can I help you?"

"We're Joe and Tanja Shepherd," I said. "We work for the sheriff's department."

She glanced back and forth between us. "I don't understand. Is there a problem?"

"Mrs. Sweet, we'd like to ask you a few questions about your daughter. We've found new evidence in the case..."

Kendra covered her mouth. "You found the killer?" she said with a slight tremor in her voice.

"Not yet," said Joe. "But we will. Can we come in?"

"Of course." She stood aside, ushering us through the doorway. As we stepped into the tiny two room cottage, I immediately noticed that the place was clean and well organized; far tidier than I would have expected based on the exterior. It was also very small. There was a kitchen to the right, a bedroom to the left, and ahead of us, a pair of French doors opened out onto a deck overlooking the river. Next to the doors, I saw a folded massage table.

"Please, have a seat," she said, gesturing towards the loveseat in the middle of the room. "Would you like some tea?"

"Yes, thank you," I said.

Joe and I settled onto the couch while Kendra started the water. A minute later, she joined us. She placed the teapot and cups on the coffee table, and took one of the chairs from the kitchen and placed it across from us. She barely had enough room for the loveseat and the single chair in the same small living room.

We went through the motions of selecting our tea from a small basket filled with a variety of organic tea bags. I went with zesty lemon. Kendra chose cinnamon sage. Joe declined.

"Mrs. Sweet," I began. "We have some questions about Becky."

"Call me Kendra."

"Kendra, can you think of anyone who might have wanted to hurt your daughter?"

"No, absolutely not," she said. "I've been through this a hundred times with the police. Becky didn't have any enemies."

"What about Jimmy Pishard?" said Joe.

"Jimmy? Oh, he wouldn't do something like that."

"Are you sure?" I said.

"Of course. We spent an entire summer with him. We went camping, canoeing, rock climbing. He used to spend the night here three or four times a week, when they were dating."

"He slept with your daughter?" I said, raising an eyebrow.

"Of course. My daughter was a mature young woman. She used birth control. It's natural for children to explore their sexuality. You'd be surprised how many people don't understand that."

"So you believe that a teenager is ready for a sexual relationship?" I said.

"Absolutely. If they're old enough to drive, to have a job, or to be drafted, they're old enough to enjoy life's pleasures as well, don't you think?"

"About Jimmy," Joe said. "Did you know that he was the primary suspect in your daughter's death?"

"I suppose so. I mean, the police kept asking me about him over and over again. I told them they were barking up the wrong tree, but you know how police can be. No offense."

"None taken," I said, glancing at Joe. "Kendra, do you know someone named Randall Rosen?"

She stared into her tea. "No... no, I don't think so. Should I?"

"It appears that on the night of her murder, your daughter wasn't alone. Randall's body was found nearby. He was killed that night, too."

Kendra set her tea on the table and laced her fingers together. "I don't understand. What does this mean?"

"It's hard to say," said Joe. "Right now, we're just trying to find out what connection he had to your daughter."

"I don't know... was he a student?"

"No," I said. "He was a reporter for the San Francisco Chronicle."

"I'm afraid I can't help you. I wish I could. Unless..."

"What is it?"

"I suppose I should start at the beginning. Becky was very young when her father died. She was very impressionable. I decided it was best to keep from her the fact that it was a suicide. Unfortunately, when she got older and eventually learned the truth, she refused to believe it. I take responsibility for that. I was trying to protect her, you must understand that."

"What happened?"

"During her senior year, Becky became obsessed with proving her father's death was a murder. She told me that she remembered him, and that he never would have done that. I tried to explain to her that sometimes people just can't cope; that sometimes they feel they can't go on anymore. She was adamant that her father would not have killed himself."

"Did your husband have emotional problems?" I said.

"Oh, no, not at all. He was actually a very happy individual. He loved us very much. The truth is that his suicide came as quite a shock to me. I suppose they always do."

I leaned forward, touching her hand. "Did your daughter have any reason for this belief? When she spoke about it, did she have any evidence?"

"She said he had promised to take her to Disneyland for her birthday, and that he would never have made that promise if he didn't plan to keep it."

"That's not really evidence," I said.

"Of course not. I tried to explain that to her, but the more I tried to convince her, the more she dug her heels in. She started talking to people he worked with, even his old high school friends. It's possible that she had gone to this Randall person for help. I don't know where else that she would have met him. Although, she did have a journalism class at school. Since he was a reporter, perhaps she met him that way."

"Thank you, Kendra. You've been a lot of help. Can we call you if we have any more questions?"

"Of course."

"Oh, and one more thing," I said. "Do you mind if I use your bathroom?"

Five minutes later, we were back in the Suburban. "That was interesting," Joe said as he pulled back onto the road. "What is she, some kind of Buddhist or something?"

"New-Ager," I said. "Did you see the crystals? The sandalwood incense, the meditation rug?"

"I guess. I was mostly looking at the Buddha statue."

"That wasn't Buddha," I said.

Joe glanced at me.

"Yes it was. The bald guy with the big belly. Buddha."

"That's Budai. He was a monk. Don't feel bad; people confuse him with the Buddha all the time."

Joe gave me a quizzical look. "You seem to know an awful lot about this stuff."

"I took a comparative religions class in college. You know what college is, Joe?"

"Never heard of it. So you're saying Kendra Sweet is *not* a Buddhist?"

"That's exactly what I'm saying. She practices New Age spiritualism. It's a religious movement with roots in eastern philosophy and pagan spiritism. They embrace a variety of different creeds and cultures. They are only loosely organized, if at all."

"Do all of these New Ager people believe in letting their kids have sex?"

"They pride themselves on open-mindedness," I said. "Joe, you do know that northern California is considered the home of the modern New Age movement, right? Where have you been all your life?"

"Working," he said with a sneer. "Have you been keeping something from me? Are you a New-Ager?"

"Hardly. If Autumn thinks I'm going to let her high school boyfriends spend the night, she's going to have another thing coming."

Joe laughed. "So tell me, FBI lady: *Was Kendra telling us the truth?*"

"I think so. The woman is scattered. I'm sure you could tell from her mannerisms that she has a history of drug use. She also has emotional problems. But I didn't notice any signs of intentional deception."

"Intentional?"

"Let me put it this way: There is a difference between lying and forgetting. In her case, I would suspect the latter first."

"So you think she may have left out something important?"

"I'm not saying that. She was helpful, I suppose."

"We should track down Becky's old journalism teacher while we're in town. He might still work at the school."

"Sounds good."

"And then we can talk about that check in your purse."

I stared at him. "You went through my purse?"

Joe looked me up and down, making some sort of mental calculation, and turned his focus back on the road. "We can talk about it later."

"You had no right."

"You had no right to go to my grandmother for money," he snapped.

I bit my lip. Tears welled up in my eyes. *Rotten hormones.* Figures they'd kick in right when I needed to be strong. I started to say something in my own defense, but cut it short as the tears came. I looked the other way. Joe stared guiltily at the road.

We finished the drive in silence.

Healdsburg High School was a sprawling campus covered in aging and dilapidated buildings and surrounded by tall chain link fences. As we crawled out of the Suburban, Joe leaned on his cane and turned his head slowly, taking it all in.

"Does it bring back memories?" I said.

"It's strange. Things are so different now, and yet somehow the same. Some of the buildings have been rejuvenated."

"They have?" I said skeptically.

"You should have seen them before. These fences... this is all new. The place looks like a penitentiary. It used to be an open campus. They must have had some problems."

"I don't see how eight foot fences are the answer. If you have to lock the kids inside, maybe the kids aren't the problem."

Joe shook his head. "I remember breaking in here a few times, just for fun. We didn't vandalize the school or anything. We were just wild kids, looking for a good time."

I cocked an eyebrow. "I think I'm beginning to see the problem."

Joe ignored me. He headed for the office, leaning on his cane as he walked. I hadn't thought about it until that moment, but his swim in the cold lake must have done a number on his hip. I suddenly felt very sorry for him, watching him ambling towards his old high school, looking more like a broken old man than a returning hero.

Everything falls apart, I thought, and had to force myself not to cry. I hurried after him.

A short woman with narrow eyes, a pinched nose, and a million freckles greeted us at the counter. Her nametag said "Linda." We introduced ourselves and I said, "We'd like to speak to your journalism teacher.

We don't have an appointment, but it will only take a few minutes."

"That would be Solomon King," she said. "Give me a moment."

She dialed King's room, and explained that two police detectives were there to see him. After hanging up, she reached into a drawer and pulled out two guest badges. "Take these," she said. "You'll find Mr. King in Room 106 down the hall."

The hallway was quiet and empty and smelled of cafeteria food. The sound of our shoes echoed around us we walked, and children's voices came drifting in from the football field. My stomach rumbled, and I tried to ignore the heartburn working its way up into my esophagus. Baby Autumn was punishing me for skipping lunch.

It didn't help that my nerves were on edge. The whole situation with Joe was hanging over my head like a storm cloud. I was furious with him for going through my purse to find that check, but I was also angry with myself for not telling him about it sooner. I wanted to explain to him that Grandma had offered the money; that I'd tried to refuse it several times, but she had insisted. I knew that if I brought it up, we'd be right back to arguing. I didn't have the energy or the emotional stamina.

When we reached the classroom, Mr. King was in the middle of a class. Rather than interrupting, we decided to wait it out. While we were standing there, a young girl with ripped up clothes and a knitted beret went skateboarding by. Naturally, Joe waved her over.

"Hey, what time does this class get out?" he said.

"Ten minutes. Then it's lunch."

"Perfect," said Joe. "Nice board. Is that a Santa Cruz?"

"Yeah, I skate old school."

"Good for you."

Joe wistfully gazed after her as the kid skated off down the hall. He turned back to me and realized I'd been staring at him.

"What?" he said.

"Did you just encourage that girl to skateboard inside the school?"

"So what?"

"Joe, it's against the rules! She wasn't even wearing a helmet for Pete's sake!"

Joe rolled his eyes at me. "Helmets are for sissies."

"Right. So says the gimp with a cane."

"I'll have you know that if it wasn't for all those years of skateboarding and biking, I might not have survived the fall off that building, in order to need this cane."

"How do you figure?"

"Because I know *how to land*," he said. "I learned how to protect my head, rather than depending on some junky piece of foam to do it for me."

I had a whole slew of statistics ready to quote back at him, but I let it go. I knew I'd never win that argument, not for a lack of facts, but because Joe would never concede. Thankfully, the bell rang and the hall immediately filled with teenagers. Joe and I waited outside for the wave of bodies to subside, and then stepped into the classroom.

We saw a tall, distinguished looking gentleman wearing wire-rimmed glasses writing on the chalkboard. He heard us come in, and placed the chalk in the tray as we approached him.

"Hello, I'm Mr. King," he said. "Linda tells me you're with the police?"

"We're private investigators, working with the Sheriff's Department," I said. "We'd like to ask you some questions about Becky Sweet. Did you teach this class when she went to school here?"

"Oh, yes, I remember her well. She's the poor girl who died a few years ago."

"Murdered, actually," Joe said. "Do you know if Becky had any enemies in school?"

"Not that I know of," Mr. King said. "I know she dated several different boys. I suppose there may have been some jealousy or rivalry, but I never saw anything that struck me as concerning."

"Did you know Randall Rosen?"

Mr. King narrowed his eyebrows and tapped his chin. "That name does sound familiar. I'm not sure I can place it."

"He was a reporter," I said. "With the San Francisco Chronicle."

He snapped his fingers. "Of course! He was a guest speaker here. Randall gave us a nice lecture about how the children could use the skills they were learning in my classroom to start a career. I had forgotten... he was here the same semester that Becky died, wasn't he? Randall didn't have something to do with her death, did he?"

"When was the last time you spoke to Randall?" I said.

"Just that once. It was part of a promotional tour for his book. We were glad to have him, of course. It's not every day that the students get to meet a real journalist, and from the *Chronicle* no less. What does all of this have to do with Becky?"

"Randall Rosen was with Becky Sweet the night she was killed," Joe said.

"Oh, my goodness." He glanced back and forth between us as he settled into his chair and tapped a pen nervously on his desk. "Randall didn't do it, did he? The truth is, I didn't know him that well. He was just a guest speaker, you see-"

"Relax," said Joe. "Randall didn't kill Becky Sweet. He was murdered the same night."

"I see... I wonder why the police never told anyone. I'm sure I would have recognized his name in the papers."

"His body was missing," I said. "It wasn't discovered until just now. That's why we need to know about Randall's relationship with Becky."

He leaned back and ran a hand through his hair. "I'm afraid that's all I know. Like I said, he only spoke here that one time. I imagine it's possible that they had connections outside the classroom, but I had no awareness of that."

"Thanks for your time, Mr. King," I said. "Can we contact you if we have any more questions?"

"Of course."

We excused ourselves, and left the room.

"That's strange," Joe said quietly as we were walking back down the hall.

"What? That Becky met Randall at school?"

"No, I mean Mr. King. I just thought he would remember me."

"Were you in his class?"

"No. I used to see him in the hallways all the time. I served detention with him a couple of times."

"Detention? Why do I have the feeling that there's a lot about your childhood you haven't told me?"

"Because there's a lot about my childhood I haven't told you." He shook his head. "It doesn't matter. I'm sure he's seen thousands of kids go through these hallways."

"There is definitely that. And I'm sure you've changed a lot."

My stomach rumbled again, and that time Joe heard it. "We'd better get you some food," he said with a laugh.

We drove across town to a nice little taqueria that Joe swore had the best super burritos in all northern California. My stomach rumbled all the way there. I was looking forward to a nice big meal, but I was not looking forward to the inevitable conversation that would follow.

I realized as we were driving that I had been focusing on Joe's snooping in my purse. That was the source of my anger. But that wasn't right at all. It was a tactic, a diversion from the real subject. It didn't matter that I hadn't specifically asked for that money, or that Grandma had practically forced it on me. What mattered was that I had kept it a secret from Joe. Just like I'd kept our imminent foreclosure a secret. In both cases, I had no right to do that, and it was time to come clean.

Joe wasn't going to like it, but he was about to learn the truth about everything.

Chapter 8

Joe

Little Joe's Tacos were every bit as good as I remembered. It was also just as noisy and even more crowded. Tanja and I had to wait for a table. Tanja took a seat on the bench in the waiting area, and I stood next to her, leaning on my cane. I didn't want to sit down for fear of my leg cramping up, and I also didn't want to stand for the same reason. The truth was that no matter what I did, it was going to hurt. I was just trying to minimize the inevitable pain.

The place smelled like heaven with extra onions, and by the time we were seated, my stomach was growling even louder than hers was. Thankfully, we had chips and salsa to snack on while we waited for our lunch.

Twice during our meal, Tanja tried to bring up Grandma's check. Both times, I changed the subject. I'd had some time to think about it, and I had realized that I was wrong. I was wrong for accusing her in the first place. Tanja had probably mentioned offhandedly that business had been slow, and Grandma had all but forced her to take the check.

That's the kind of thing Grandma does. She's very maternal, very protective of her family. As tactful as Tanja is, she probably didn't have the heart to flat-out refuse the offer. Most likely, she had just taken the check to get Grandma off the subject. Tanja hadn't mentioned it to me yet, because we'd been so busy. Maybe she had been planning to tear the thing up anyway.

Unfortunately, I hadn't figured all of this out until *after* I had made my wife cry. I had been hating on myself ever since. If there's any rule to manhood, it's that you don't hurt the people you love. You just don't. Making Tanja cry made me feel about as big as a gnat. I could barely bring myself to look her in the eye, much less discuss what had happened. So every time she brought it up, I changed the subject back to work.

"We know how Becky and Randall met," I said at one point. "I just don't understand what they were doing together at the dairy."

"It could have been a romance," said Tanja. "With her being underage, perhaps they were meeting in secret."

"I doubt that. Her mother used to let Jimmy Pishard spend the night, remember? Randall would have had no reason to sneak around like that."

"Unless he was married, and didn't want it to get out."

"That's possible," I said. "Either way, it brings us back to the question of who killed them, and why."

"Could have been any of a dozen different boyfriends," said Tanja. "It sounds like her love life was fairly active."

"Maybe, but only one of them panned out as a suspect."

"Jimmy? He wasn't much of a suspect. If Jimmy really was the genius super-villain the cops made him out to be, I doubt he'd be working at a junkyard, and living in a trailer."

"Good point," I admitted grudgingly. "If anything, he's just a burnout. He used his experiences as an excuse to give up on life."

"Then we're in agreement?" she said. "We're crossing Jimmy off the list?"

"Might as well. There is another interesting possibility, though."

"What's that?"

I smiled. "What other psychopath do we know who's involved in this case and capable of murder?"

"You're thinking of Jimmy's father," Tanja said. "I suppose that's possible, but what would be his motive? The police never made any connection between James Pishard and Becky Sweet. And wouldn't Jimmy have said something, if that was the case?"

"Hard to say. Unless they did it together."

"Now that is far fetched," she said. "They hated each other. James Pishard has no connection to this case other than the fact that his son was a suspect."

"Okay, let's rule both of them out for now. Where does that leave us?"

"We have ex-boyfriends, most of whom probably don't even live here anymore. We have Randall Rosen, whose only connection at this point is that journalism class-" Her phone rang, cutting her off. "It's Diekmann," she said as she glanced at the screen.

She took the call. Normally, Tanja would have left the restaurant to avoid disturbing the other patrons. Today, there wasn't any point. The taqueria was as noisy as a football stadium, and almost as crowded. I could see three people talking on their phones just in our vicinity, and all three were struggling to communicate over the cacophony of noise and music playing in the background. Nobody was going to be offended by another loud conversation in that place.

I stroked my goatee as I stared out the window, waiting. A minute later, Tanja hung up. "Diekmann located a missing persons report on Randall Rosen from five years ago. His wife Caroline filed it. Get this: when Caroline filed the report, she told the police she thought her husband was having an affair."

I raised an eyebrow. "Sounds like she had a motive."

"Uh-huh, except Diekmann already contacted her by phone, and she has an alibi. Caroline was out of the country the night Randall and Becky were killed."

"Okay," I said. "So what now?"

"I can only think of one other person who might have known what was going on in Randall's life."

"Who?" I said. "His boss? We have an appointment to meet him tomorrow."

"Nope," Tanja said. "His literary agent."

My eyes widened. Until she mentioned it, I had completely forgotten that Randall had been on a book tour at the time of the murders. "Okay. Who's the agent?"

"I don't know," Tanja said, tapping the screen of her cell phone. "But give me five minutes."

I admit doubting her as I watched Tanja scroll through pages of internet search results, but in less than five minutes, she proved me wrong. She proudly held up the phone, displaying the website of a San Francisco literary agent named Natalie Brown. A carousel of books that she represented was on the front page. Randall's was among them.

"Impressive," I said.

Tanja dialed the contact information. A minute later, she hung up. "Natalie can't see us today, and she won't talk over the phone. She wants to check our credentials and verify who we are. I told her she could contact the sheriff."

"So what now? We just wait?"

"She made an appointment for us tomorrow morning. Once she's satisfied that we are who we say we are, she'll find the files for us."

"I guess that means we have the afternoon off," I said, smiling.

"Perfect. You can fix that cabinet door I've been asking about for two weeks. And we can talk about a few things."

I groaned. "I think I need a drink."

"No you don't. You're driving. And you're stuck with it until I can fit behind the wheel again."

The waitress returned with our receipt. I signed the restaurant's copy, and scribbled in a tip. As I set the pen down, I had the terrible feeling that I'd just spent the last of our money on nachos and super burritos. I crossed my arms on the table, leaned forward, and gazed into Tanja's mesmerizing hazel eyes. They were very dark that afternoon, and I wondered if their color was reflecting her mood. She stared back at me, expressionless.

"All right," I said. "How bad is it?"

She took a deep breath. "Our house payment is three weeks late."

I considered that. "There's some kind of grace period, right? I mean, it's not technically late until after that."

"That was three weeks ago, Joe. When I say it's late, I mean *Late,* with a capital *L.*"

I dropped my head into my hands, feeling the sharp stubble of my scalp biting into my palms. "What's going to happen?"

"That depends. I know you won't like this, but I do have Grandma's check. That will catch us up through the end of the month."

"Grandma knows all about this?" I groaned.

"What was I supposed to do, lie to her?"

"Did you have to tell her anything?"

"I'm sorry, Joe. She asked about our financial situation and I started to cry. It's not my fault. It's the hormones."

I still had my head in my hands. I looked up into her face, and she said, "Are you going to be okay?"

"I don't know. I just hate the fact that we're this close to success, and it's all falling apart around us. First, we had James Pishard trying to sue us, then Grandma's *relationship* with the sheriff, and now a foreclosure? I feel like I'm up the creek without a paddle. You know the one I'm talking about."

Tanja took my hand. "It's all going to work out, Joe. You just need to have a little faith. This is what we've been working and praying for. It's going to happen. With this check, we'll be all caught up, and after we solve a couple cases..."

"Candy will rain from heaven?" I said.

Tanja smiled. "Maybe."

Maybe. Or, maybe we'll miss the next payment too, and be living on the street just in time for the baby's arrival...

Our meeting with Randall's agent the next morning was early, so we had no choice but to make the morning commute into the city with a million or so other drivers. I had brought my cane along with me because the weather was cool and foggy, and my leg had been stiff ever since I touched that lake.

As we entered Marin county, I saw the fog thickening up, and knew it was going to be a rough day. By the time we reached the Golden Gate bridge, it was so dense and dark it may as well have been nighttime, and a dull throbbing pain started building in my hip.

Traffic jammed up in all the usual places, but thankfully there were no accidents. We managed to walk into the agent's office building a whole five minutes early for our nine o'clock appointment. We took the elevator to the twentieth floor and introduced ourselves to the intern, a longhaired college kid with a nose ring and a tribal tattoo on his neck. He buzzed his boss on the phone and said, "Mrs. Brown will see you now, you can go in."

Natalie's waiting room was tiny compared to her office, which could have served as a studio apartment. She must have spent a small fortune on the interior design. Between the mahogany furniture, the leather sofa, and the paintings, I had to wonder how much of their money her clients were seeing.

As we entered, Natalie rose up from behind her desk. She was a tall, refined looking woman with curly auburn hair, large rectangular spectacles, and a long, slightly crooked nose. She was dressed expensively, and wore more than her share of jewelry. She didn't offer us a seat, and I got the impression she wanted to get us out of there quickly.

"I spoke with Sheriff Diekmann last night," she said. Her voice was deep and earthy with a slight grittiness to it, almost masculine. "He explained the situation and verified your identities. So now that we have that out of the way, let's get down to business. How can I help you?"

"We'd like Randall Rosen's itinerary for the time surrounding his death," Tanja said. "We need to know where he was, and for how long."

"I have it on file. I'll email it to you directly. Anything else?"

"How well did you know Randall?" I said.

"As well as I know any other business partner," she said. "We had a few lunches. I know that he was married. I've been sending his widow royalty checks since he disappeared. She inherited his estate, of course."

"Do you think he might have been having an affair?" Tanja said.

Natalie's right hand went to her necklace, and she began casually stroking the pendant between her thumb and forefinger. I had no idea what it meant, but I saw that Tanja noticed it, too.

"We didn't talk about things like that," she said. "Our relationship was strictly professional."

"Of course," Tanja said quickly. "Did he mention a speaking appointment at Healdsburg High School?"

She tilted her head sideways and stared into the distance. "Now that you mention it, yes, I remember that. In fact, he called me the night of that engagement and told me to keep the presses warm."

"Meaning?" said Tanja.

"It usually means that a writer has a new book on the way, and he expects it to be a hot commodity."

"Did he say what the book was about?"

"No. I assumed it was another piece of investigative journalism. He had dreams of winning a Pulitzer someday."

"Were you sleeping with him?" said Tanja.

Natalie narrowed her eyes. "I already told you, we had a professional relationship. Now if you don't have any more questions, I have a lot of work to do."

"Thanks for your time Mrs. Brown," said Tanja.

As soon as we were back in the elevator, I turned to Tanja. "That was blunt," I said. "What made you think she was having an affair with Randall?"

"When she said her relationship with Randall was professional, did you see the way she covered her throat?" Tanja said.

"Did that mean she was lying?"

"Possibly. That movement was a tell for her discomfort. Body language like that doesn't originate in the conscious mind. It comes from the subconscious; the mammalian brain. It's the same part of our brain that tells us to defend ourselves from an attack, or in some cases, to flee. It's instinct. Natalie was touching her throat, the place where voice originates. She may have been having an affair with Randall, or she may have had knowledge of another affair. Either way, she didn't like talking about it."

"And the other arm, crossing over her body?"

Tanja grinned at me. "You've been paying attention, haven't you?"

"I'm learning."

"That's another sign that she was uncomfortable with the subject matter. It's called an unconscious blocking movement. The brain instinctively tries to protect itself. Like the way you throw your arms out when you fall, or when someone throws a football at you."

"That's not subconscious," I said.

"Not entirely, but that's because you're expecting it. The fact that you can marry your conscious goals with your subconscious reactions is what makes you so good at sports."

"Not so much anymore," I said, holding up my cane.

"You still have your days," she said with a wink. "Not all sports happen on the field. Anyway, it's nearly impossible to gauge whether a subject is lying based on body language alone. The best trick is to create a baseline of behavior. Ask questions that the subject is comfortable with, but pepper the interview with questions that are more probing. If the subject reacts in a similar fashion to one particular line of questions, you can be sure you're witnessing a pattern. Then you hammer it home until you get a confession."

"You Feds," I said, laughing.

She cocked an eyebrow. "Yes?"

"You just remind me of the men in black, acting all spooky and mysterious. No wonder you freak people out, with all your head games."

"You asked," she said.

I apologized for hurting her feelings, but she waved off my concern. "It doesn't hurt to have a reputation for being devious and clever," she said with a laugh. "In fact, it makes my job easier. When people are nervous, they slip up."

"Do you believe Randall and Becky were having an affair or not?"

"That would be almost impossible to prove. I think we should call Becky's mom again. See if Becky had a diary or journal. Even an old email address. Something to give us some insight into what was going on in her life."

"We still have one more thing to do while we're in the city," I said.

"We're not going to Chinatown so you can buy nunchakus."

"That's not what I was thinking. We have an appointment at the Chronicle, remember?"

"Right. We should probably head in that direction."

"Perfect. And after that, we can go to Chinatown and buy some nunchakus."

We parked in a garage a few blocks from the Chronicle on Mission Street. "I hope they validate," Tanja said. "Thirty-five dollars for a half hour? These rates are extortionate."

"You mean like the price of gas?" I said sarcastically. "Welcome to the new millennium."

A few minutes later, we stepped inside the San Francisco Chronicle's main office and found ourselves facing a huge room full of cubicles and desks. To our right, a girl in her late teens -probably an intern- looked up from her computer and said, "Can I help you find someone?"

Tanja told her about our appointment, and the intern picked up her phone. "Brian, the police are here to see you."

"We're not technically police," I said as she hung up. "We just work for them."

"I know," she said, smiling. "I just couldn't pass up the chance to tell Brian that the police want to talk to him."

A tall black man wearing slacks and a cardigan came hurrying in our direction. "I'm Brian Lewis, the chief editor," he said as he joined us. "How can I help you?"

"We called last night," Tanja said. "We'd like to ask a few questions about an ex-employee of yours."

"Ah, you must be the investigators from Sequoia." A sense of relief washed over his features. "Please, come into my office. This way."

He led us into an eight by ten office at the back of the building. It was less than impressive, especially considering he was the editor of a major newspaper.

"Sorry, we don't have much space anymore," he said. "It's all digital now. Computers and cubicles. One of these days, they'll figure out how to upload our brains into a computer, and there won't be any offices left at all."

"We're fine," Tanja said reassuringly. "I'm sure you're very busy, so we won't take much of your time."

"I spoke with your sheriff yesterday," Brian said, gesturing for us to sit. "I was sorry to hear about Randall. You must understand of course, that after being missing so long, it wasn't entirely unexpected. His wife had him declared dead three years ago."

"We understand she had been considering divorce before his death," Tanja said. A slight smile turned up the corners of his mouth.

"I don't doubt that. They were both very young. I don't think their marriage turned out to be what her and Randall wanted it to be."

"Do you think he might have cheated on her?" I said.

"Think? I know it for a fact. We used to go out drinking on Fridays and Randall would pick up girls right in front of us, still wearing his wedding ring! The guy was shameless. He was good, but shameless."

"I see," Tanja said. "Do you know Natalie Brown, his literary agent?"

Brian's smile vanished. "We've crossed paths a few times."

"Do you think they were having an affair?"

"It wouldn't surprise me. All I know for sure is that she kept filling his head with all these grand ideas, and that's probably what got him killed."

"What sort of ideas?"

"Oh, the usual stuff. Randall was talented, anyone could see that. He was young, energetic, and good-looking. Natalie was trying to make him into a big literary star. She had these ideas about breaking a big story and selling the movie and publishing rights. Which is a load of nonsense, of course. Big stories don't get made into movies, they get you killed."

Tanja frowned. "What do you mean?"

He leaned forward, lacing his fingers together on the desk. "Big stories always involve corruption. Usually, they involve politicians or big corporations; people with power, resources, and enough motivation to kill to protect their interests. If something like that becomes a movie, you're talking twenty or thirty years after the fact."

"You think Randall may have been working on something like that?"

"Absolutely. A few days before he disappeared, he told me he was about to break the big one. He said I'd have to visit him in Hollywood after the story got out. Then, big surprise, Randall went missing and nobody ever heard from him again."

"Do you have access to any of his records?" Tanja said. "If we had a better idea of the story he was working on..."

"I'm afraid I can't help you. It doesn't work that way. Freelance reporters like Randall do most of their work on their own computers. When the story is ready, they usually submit it to me by email. Until that point, we have nothing in our system."

I glanced at Tanja. "He must have had a laptop," I said. "Perhaps his wife would still have it."

"Doubtful," said Brian. "Randall would have had it with him. Can you imagine a writer going anywhere without his laptop?"

"We didn't find anything like that in the car," said Tanja.

"It could be at the bottom of the reservoir," I said. I instantly remembered that murky ice-cold water and regretted even thinking it.

"Don't worry," Tanja said, reading the look on my face. "I won't make you scrape the bottom of that lake again. Besides, even if we had found it, I doubt it would do us any good. Not after five years under water." She turned her attention back to Brian. "Thank you for your help, Mr. Lewis."

"Of course. If you have any more questions, feel free to call me."

In order to get our parking ticket validated, Tanja and I had to go to a nearby deli for lunch. It was the cheapest thing we could find, and considerably cheaper than the seventy dollars we'd have had to pay for parking. I didn't mind. It was turning out to be a nice day in the city. The sun had begun to burn through the fog, and my leg was glad for the chance to rest and soak up the warmth. After sitting on the patio for twenty minutes, the pain was almost gone.

While we ate, Tanja pulled the case file out of her handbag and began flipping through the pages. "What are you looking for?" I said.

"I don't know. I'm just trying to figure out what the connection was between Randall and Becky. Do you remember what her mother said about Becky's conspiracy theory about her father's death? I wonder if Randall knew about it."

"That's possible," I said. "She may have gone to him with her story."

"Could be, but the practical part of my mind tells me they were just sleeping together."

"Maybe it was both," I said. "She was a pretty girl. Definitely Randall's type. Maybe she went to him with her theory, and he promised to help because he was hoping to get her into bed."

Tanja stared at me. "You really think just like a man, you know that?"

"I am a man."

"If you ever cheat on me, I'll castrate you."

"I know, sweetness. If I was that kind of guy, I wouldn't still be around."

Tanja tilted her head slightly, as if a new thought had occurred to her. "That's right, you wouldn't be, would you?"

"Huh?"

"If you were a guy like Randall, you'd have split the second I got knocked up."

"Yeah, but I'm not."

"I know that, Joe. I'm not talking about you. I'm talking about Randall."

"I'm not following."

She let out an exasperated sigh and leaned forward. "Let's say Randall went along with Becky just to get into bed with her. A person like that would have had his fun and moved on, but he didn't. He stuck around. He told everyone he was about to break the

112

story of a lifetime. He *must* have been talking about Becky's father."

"You think he believed her story?" I said.

"He must have. It's the only thing that makes sense."

"If that's true, she must have had some pretty convincing evidence."

"Enough evidence to convince a big shot San Francisco reporter to investigate."

We stared at each other for a second. Inspiration struck, and Tanja's eyes lit up at the same time as mine.

"If they were investigating that suicide together..." I started.

"Whoever killed Becky and Randall also killed Becky's father!"

She closed the file and put it back in the briefcase. "I think it's time for another talk with Becky's mother."

Chapter 9

Tanja

Before we left the city, I called Kendra Sweet to ask whether her daughter had kept a diary or a journal. Kendra wasn't sure, but she invited us to stop by and go through Becky's old things. I was convinced that Becky's relationship with Randall was what had gotten him killed, but there was some piece of the puzzle that was still missing.

Was it really possible that Becky's father had been murdered? Had Richard Sweet been involved in some sort of scandal or crime? Did her investigation into his death lead to her own, and Randall's as well?

I mulled these questions over during our drive back home, but reached no conclusions. Eventually, my thoughts turned back to personal problems and I remembered something I'd been meaning to ask Joe.

"Diekmann said something strange on the phone earlier," I said.

"What's that?"

"He wanted to know if you'd made that call yet."

Joe fixed his gaze straight ahead. He cleared his throat. "What call?"

"He didn't say. I thought you would know what he meant."

Joe shrugged. "Who knows? Maybe he meant the phone call you just made."

"I doubt it," I said firmly. "Diekmann didn't know we'd be talking to Kendra Sweet."

"I wouldn't worry about it."

I pulled my gaze away from him and pretended to be web surfing on my phone. "Are you keeping something from me, Joe?"

"Yes. I'm actually a millionaire. I just pretend to be poor so I can be sure you really love me."

"You don't have to get snarky."

"Why don't you just drop it?"

I let out a big, exasperated sigh. "Fine. I won't bring it up anymore."

An hour and a half later, we were back at Kendra Sweet's mountainside cottage. Kendra was just finishing up with one of her clients, a dark-haired woman who smelled like cinnamon-scented massage oil as she brushed by us on the porch.

Kendra appeared in the doorway and invited us in. It was dark inside -save for a dozen burning candles- and soothing music drifted out of the stereo system. Smoke curled up from an incense stick on the mantle. She had pushed the loveseat out of the middle of the room to make room for a massage table.

"Just give me a minute," Kendra said as she flicked on the lights. She scurried about the room, dousing candles and opening up the shades. Joe helped her fold the massage table back up.

"Betty is one of my regular clients," Kendra said apologetically. "Otherwise, I would have cancelled because I knew you were coming. I hope you don't mind."

"Not at all," I said.

She carried the massage table over to the wall, and Joe helped her put the couch back in place. He had left his cane in the car, and I saw him wince, but he tried to put on a tough façade.

"All right," Kendra said. "You asked about journals?"

"Yes, or anything that might give us an idea what Becky was investigating about her father's death."

She considered that. "There's an old box I keep in the attic. It has some of her things..." she began wandering towards the bedroom as she spoke. "Becky had a collection of things from her father. She had added some articles about his death to the collection, and I didn't care for it, because I thought it was morbid, but I figured it would help her get over her obsession. She just needed to move on, you know?"

Joe and I followed Kendra into her bedroom. She opened the closet, pulled out a stepladder, and pushed open a trap door to the attic. "Can you hold the ladder?" she called down as she poked her head through the hole in the ceiling. Joe stabilized the ladder as Kendra reached into the attic and began rummaging through her things. A blanket fell down, grazing Joe's head on the way to the floor, followed by an empty duffel bag and a stuffed animal.

"Here it is!" she said at last. She struggled to maneuver a cardboard box through the hole as she climbed back down the ladder. I took it from her, and Joe helped her safely back to the floor.

"I don't know what we'll find in there," she said. "After Becky's death, I sort of shoved everything in that box. At the time, I couldn't deal with it. It's hard, you know? Losing someone so close to you. When Richard died, at least I still had Becky..." Her voice cracked, and she trailed off.

"I can't imagine how difficult all of this must have been for you," I said.

She dabbed a tissue at her eyes and then straightened up, trying to regain her composure.

"All right, let's have a look," she said after a moment.

Kendra took the box from me and led the way back to the kitchen. She placed it on the table and began pulling out the contents. First came a set of pom-poms, and then an old .mp3 player. She pulled out a scrapbook, and handed it to me.

I flipped through the first few pages and saw a number of clippings from the local paper about her father's death, including an obituary. There was an old photograph of two young men in swimming shorts, bodies tanned and glistening with water, arms draped over each other's shoulders.

"That's Richard on the right," Kendra said. "That photo was taken when we were in high school. That was before digital cameras. Can you remember those days?"

"Just barely," said Joe.

"Who is Richard's friend?" I said.

She glanced at the photo. "That's James Pishard. Those two were thick as thieves in the old days."

"Pishard?" I said, glancing at Joe. He leaned over for a closer look.

"That's him all right. What do you make of that?"

"Coincidence?" I said in an unconvincing tone. I noticed Kendra's perplexed look. I explained. "Joe and I didn't realize you knew Jimmy Pishard's father."

"Oh, all the families are connected around this town," Kendra said. "I see people from high school every time I go to the grocery store."

I flipped the page, and found several more pictures of Richard and Pishard. I saw another I didn't recognize. "Who's this?" I said.

Kendra leaned closer. "That's strange... I have no idea. I don't believe I've ever seen that young man before."

I pulled the photo out and flipped it over. A name was scribbled on the back. "Myles Meyer, nineteen eighty-nine. Ring a bell?"

"I don't think so..."

I flipped the page and found a newspaper article. The title read: *"Local boy missing."* Under the title was a black and white photo of Myles. "This article is from nineteen ninety," I said. I turned the page and another article declared:

"Police call off search for missing teen."

"I don't get it," Joe said. "Who is Myles Meyer? Why is he in this book?"

"I remember now!" Kendra exclaimed. "He was a new boy, from out of town. He only lived here a few weeks. I never even realized that he was missing. I just assumed he moved away. That happens sometimes, usually in military families. How terrible. I never realized what had happened... He was cute, you know. I remember all the girls had a crush on him."

"I wonder if he was ever found," I said. I flipped to the next page and found it empty. The article on Myles was the last thing in the scrapbook.

"We can check the sheriff's records tomorrow," Joe said.

118

I picked up Becky's old .mp3 player and turned it on. The battery was dead. "Do you mind if I borrow this?" I said.

"I suppose. Please be careful with it, though. I don't have many things of Becky's left."

"I promise. I'll get it back to you as soon as possible."

As soon as we got home, I dug through the kitchen drawers and found some spare batteries for the .mp3 player. It seemed to be working, so I grabbed a pair of headphones and told Joe I was going for a walk. He looked at me as if I was crazy.

"It's almost dinnertime."

"Relax, I won't be gone long. Defrost a salmon while I'm gone." His face lit up at the word *salmon*. I rolled my eyes. "I'm the one who's pregnant."

"Sympathy hunger."

"Uh-huh."

There was a chill wind blowing up the street as I stepped outside. I saw a wall of fog creeping in from the coast, and dark storm clouds loomed overhead. Our brief respite from the winter storms was just about over, it seemed. I paused to zip up my hoodie. My belly looked like a basketball under the fabric.

I put the headphones on, pressed play, and began to walk.

"Friday the 23rd," Becky's voice began. *"I spoke with the county coroner's office about my father's death. They were no help..."*

My heart skipped a beat. I had been hoping the .mp3 player might have some clue on it as to what had been going on in Becky's life, but I didn't dare hope she had been using it as a journal. I continued walking, slightly light headed from the rush of excitement.

"I'm looking into the connections between my father's death and other incidents that may be related..."

Becky's dictation went on to describe her conversations with a number of people in regards to her father's death. Among those, she had interviewed one of the deputies who had been at the death scene. She had also spoken to several of her father's friends and co-workers, and the storeowner from the shop where the gun he used to commit suicide was purchased.

The first few were no help at all, but the last one was curious because the storeowner didn't recognize the picture of her father. Becky asked to see the storeowner's records so she could verify who the buyer was, but he declined, citing the need to protect his customer's rights. Dismissed as a nosey teen, Becky had no recourse.

I made a mental note to ask Diekmann about that. It didn't surprise me that his deputies hadn't looked too deeply into the origin of the gun, because at the time, no one suspected foul play. No one except a young impressionable girl, that is. It was strange, listening to that ghostly recording. I couldn't help shivering as I thought about the fact that Becky was speaking to me from beyond the grave. This young girl, so full of hope and strength, didn't *exist* anymore. She was *gone,* cut down in the prime of her youth, murdered by some maniac who'd beat her over the head and left her to drown in a vat of cream.

I silently promised myself that I was going to find out who had done this to Becky. She deserved that much. She deserved justice for what had happened. I turned right at the end of the street, and followed the sidewalk along the western edge of the park, hoping the trees would help cut the wind.

As I walked, I listened to Becky's vibrant young voice describing details of her interactions with a dozen different people. I sympathized with her as she came up empty-handed time after time. I could hear the strain in her tone, the frustration of butting her head against a wall that wouldn't budge. At times, she sounded so despondent that I wanted to cry for her.

Yet she persisted. Becky was thoroughly convinced of her father's murder. She held that belief with a stubborn conviction that I could only shake my head at and admire. At one point, she recited the details of her conversations with Randall Rosen. According to her voice-diary, Becky had never met the reporter until the day he spoke at her school. Sensing an opportunity, she had cornered him in the stadium and begged him to listen to her tale. He had been reluctant at first, but there must have been something about her beauty or her obstinacy that convinced him to hear her out.

Becky recounted their conversation, and details of a second meeting that they were going to have, but she never finished the recording. At the end of the file, I expected Becky's voice to return, but instead the sound of heavy breathing filled my ears.

I heard footsteps and the sounds of cracking branches. I stopped in my tracks and a chill ran down my spine. I turned, monitoring the dark woods around me as I listened.

At last, I heard a voice. It was Becky:

"I knew you would come," she said. Her voice sounded muffled, distant, as if she'd kept the recorder hidden secret in her pocket.

"What made you so sure?" said a man's voice.

"Because I know what you did."

"You don't know what you're talking about."

"I can't prove it yet, but I will."

"Listen to me, kid," the man's voice rose to an angry shout. "I know about you and that reporter friend of yours. You've been asking questions all around town. I came to tell you to stop, if you know what's good for you."

"Or what? You'll kill me, too?"

"Drop it, kid. I'm warning you."

"I know about that boy. I know you killed him, just like you killed my dad."

"If you keep talking like that, you'll end up just like them. I won't-"

The conversation ended, and after a minute of wind and rustling noises, the recording shut off. I pulled the recorder out of my pocket and saw that I had reached the end of the last file.

Darkness had fallen while I walked, and I stared up through the trembling canopy of trees into the swirling mass of black clouds overhead. Off to my left, deep and impenetrable shadows covered the redwood grove. It was almost pitch black in there, and eerily silent. Being under the redwoods is like being closed off to the rest of the world. The weather doesn't touch you, the light doesn't touch you...

Lightning flashed, arcing over the hills with such brilliance that it momentarily blinded me. I stood there, counting the seconds just the way I had learned as a child, until at last, the thunder came rolling across town, shaking windows and setting off car alarms. I don't know where I stopped counting, because something else was on my mind:

122

Becky knew the killer. She had actually spoken to him!

But who was it? She had accused the man of slaying her father and someone else. I could only presume she meant the boy from the article, Myles Meyer. If I'd been listening right, it sure seemed like the man had confessed to both. At the very least, he had warned her from that line of inquiry under the threat of physical injury. Whoever it was, the guy was a real psychopath.

What was I thinking? Of course he was! The man was guilty of murdering a young boy! Not just that, but also Becky's father, and then framing it up like a suicide... and he had committed the double murders of Becky and Randall to cover it all up. My heart skipped a beat.

The voice on the recording was *a serial killer!*

My head was spinning. I turned back the way I had come, hurrying to beat the rain if I could. I left the trail, taking a shortcut straight through the park. As I walked, a light mist began to fall. I wanted to break into a run, but with my luck I knew I'd trip and fall, and probably hurt myself. It would be just like me to break my water and give birth to Autumn right there in the park. Even if that didn't happen, I'd be in trouble if I fell and twisted my ankle in my condition.

I made a conscious effort to slow down, fixing my eyes on the ground to avoid any obstacles waiting to trip me up in the darkness. A flash of headlights up ahead caught my attention, and a sedan came around the corner at the end of the street. The tires screeched as they broke traction on the wet pavement. The driver regained control and slowed, moving more cautiously.

To my surprise, the vehicle came to a stop in front of our house with the engine running.

I frowned, trying to remember if I knew anyone with a car like that. As I pondered that question, a shadowy figure stepped out of the driver's door and stood facing the house. I heard the double click of a shotgun shell entering the chamber, followed by the explosive combustion of a gunshot. Our living room window exploded.

"Joe!" I screamed. I broke into a run. The man pumped the action and fired again, and then a third time.

I tripped and fell to my knees, and a searing pain ripped through my abdomen. The sound of my cries was drowned out by the violent bursts of gunfire.

It went on for several seconds. Seven shots. Seven seconds of excruciating pain and blinding terror. I pushed to my feet and stumbled again as the man turned, tossing the shotgun into the backseat. He crawled into the car, revved the engine up, and squealed the tires as he went racing down the street. Within seconds, it was all over.

I was screaming as I reached the edge of the park, both arms wrapped around my belly as if I could somehow hold the baby inside of me. I fixed my gaze on what remained of the living room window. Shards of glass stuck out like misshapen icicles, and the curtains whipped in the wind. I could clearly see the painting of a sailboat on the far wall, the broken frame and shattered glass hanging by the wire.

I had the sudden horrible sensation that the body of my husband was on the floor inside that room. For all I knew, he might be bleeding to death that very second. The front door flew open, and Joe came racing towards me. I was so relieved that my knees went weak and I nearly fell down a second time.

Joe crossed the street in a flash and caught me up in his arms, pulling me close, nearly lifting me off the ground as the warmth of his embrace washed over me. I heard sirens wailing in the distance. I pressed my face into Joe's shoulder and wept.

"It's okay," he whispered into my ear. "I'm okay. It's going to be okay."

"Who was that?" I said, my voice muffled by his shirt. "Why would someone do that?"

"I don't know, but I'm going to find out."

I felt a sharp pain in my abdomen, and I grunted. "Joe, I have to sit down. Help me."

He bent over and swooped my legs out from under me. He carried me a few yards down the sidewalk and set me gently on a bench, the pain in his hip completely forgotten in his rush of adrenaline and fear. He laid his hand on my belly, and gave me a look of grave concern.

"The baby?" he said.

"She's okay... I think so anyway."

"Just sit still. The police will be here any second. We'll call for an ambulance." Joe ran back to the house to fetch a blanket for me, and returned just as the first squad car arrived.

Diekmann showed up while the paramedics were checking me out. He knelt down next to me. "Are you okay?"

"Shook up," I said. "Thankfully, my water didn't break."

"Do the two of you have any idea who might have done this?"

"James Pishard," Joe said without hesitation.

"The guy who threatened to sue you?"

"Yep. I'm sure it was him."

"You saw him?"

"It was too dark. I didn't get a clear look at him, but it's the only thing that makes sense. He started making trouble from the moment he found out we were on this case."

The paramedics loaded me onto a gurney. Diekmann asked them to give us a second. He turned his gaze on me

"How about you? Did you see the shooter?"

"I'm afraid not," I said. "Joe's right about Pishard, though. The man is a psychopath."

"All right," said Diekmann. "I'll send a couple deputies to bring him in for questioning. Joe, you go ahead with Tanja to the hospital. I'll call you if we find him."

They loaded me into the ambulance and Joe settled onto the narrow bench next to me. Diekmann stood in the opening behind us.

"Take care of her, Joe. I'm gonna get the S.O.B. who did this."

"Not if I find him first," Joe said.

Diekmann slammed the doors shut, and the ambulance pulled away with Diekmann barking orders about photographing everything and collecting the shells for evidence.

Chapter 10

Joe

I'm not the murdering type. I may have broken some bones in my time, but at least a few of them were my own. I admit, I've been tempted to take the law into my own hands, especially when standing face to face with some sleazy scumbag who I knew was responsible for unforgivable crimes, but even at times like that, I've kept my cool. Mostly.

I've learned to stare into the eyes of drug dealers, murderers, and God only knows what else, and smile as if I was one of them. That's what it took to survive. I always told myself justice would catch up with them eventually. Maybe even karma. But there are some lines you just don't cross. I've been through all sorts of dangerous situations, and never once felt the kind of pure, unbridled rage that I felt that night.

When I heard that first gunshot, and the sound of my living room window exploding into a million shards of glass, my thoughts immediately went to Tanja. Even as the shotgun slugs hammered into the sheetrock just inches away from my head, I was thinking about her.

I dove to the living room floor and felt bits and pieces of glass and sheetrock raining down on me. I pushed to my hands and knees, and the broken glass sliced into my palms like razor blades. I dismissed the pain and ignored the repeated thundering *kabooms* as I crawled out of the living room and headed straight down the hall. I reached the bedroom and pulled my Colt .45 out from under the mattress.

Tanja hates that. She says I need to get a gun safe before Autumn is born. I will, of course, when I absolutely have to. Until then, I want my gun accessible. In the end, no one but me is responsible for the safety and well-being of my family. If something terrible happens that I could have prevented, no one else will share that burden. How does the old saying go? *I'd rather be judged by twelve than carried by six.* That's my philosophy now. When I do lock my gun up, I'm going to find a safe that I can open in half a second, even in the dark.

I was back up the hall in seconds, locked and loaded. The shooter seemed to have focused his attention on the living room. Between firings, I slipped around the corner and into the kitchen. From there, I had a clear view through the kitchen window. He was little more than a silhouette, obscured by the rain and backlit by the headlights of his car. I trained my sights on him. My finger was already squeezing the trigger when I saw the shadow of movement in the park behind him.

At that point, I couldn't even be sure it was Tanja. I could only tell that a civilian had come into my line of fire. I had to move. I lowered my 1911 and backed around the table, looking for a clear shot. As I moved, the shrubs at the corner of the porch obscured my view of the scene. I still couldn't get a shot.

I was tempted to run out the side door and around the front of the house, but I didn't want to take my eyes off the shooter. I considered jumping through the kitchen window. I might get a clear shot when I hit the front lawn. Before I had a chance, the shooter tossed his shotgun in the car and took off like a rocket.

I ran out the front door and saw Tanja on her knees at the edge of the park across the street. For a second, the whole world froze. My guts wrenched up like a busted spring and I instantly assumed the worst. She'd been hit. My wife and baby had been shot...

I crossed the thirty yards between us in about three steps.

A few hours later, the doctor -a young Indian woman with a thin face and a large smile- gave us the test results. "I'm Doctor Sharma," she said with a strong accent. "I want you to know that your sonogram was clear and everything looks fine."

I took a deep, relieved breath.

"What about the pain?" Tanja said. "I thought I felt something tearing."

Dr. Sharma lifted the front of Tanja's gown and felt around her belly. Tanja winced as she touched a spot.

"That is what I expected," the doctor said. "You most likely strained a muscle. You're in a very late stage of pregnancy and things are moving around in there constantly, stretching, trying to make space for the baby. Whatever you felt, it wasn't anything dangerous. Our tests have shown that you and Autumn are perfectly healthy. There's no sign of internal stress or bleeding."

"Thank goodness," Tanja said. "Can we go home?"

"I'd prefer to keep you overnight, just for observation. We'll release you in the morning. In the meanwhile, get some rest. From now on, no strenuous activity: no exercise, no jogging, nothing like that. You can walk, but take it easy. Your baby has two more weeks before the due date, so let's not rush anything."

We thanked her, and the doctor left us alone. Tanja turned the television up, and for a while, we were quiet. Unfortunately, I couldn't stop thinking about what had happened. My adrenaline was high, and now that I knew Tanja and the baby were safe, I wanted to get out there and find the guy who'd done this.

I kept glancing out the window, knowing he was out there somewhere, and feeling helpless and frustrated just sitting there in that hospital room. And more than a little claustrophobic. At one point, I began to pace, and Tanja guessed what I was thinking:

"Joe, don't leave. Stay here with me, please... I don't want to be alone."

I settled onto the bed next to her. "He's out there somewhere," I said. "The piece of trash shot at my house. He could have killed any one of us."

"I know that, Joe, but I don't want you to go after him alone. Just wait until we hear from Diekmann, okay?"

I sighed. It was the look on her face that made up my mind. I wouldn't leave her. I couldn't. If I left my wife alone and afraid on a night like that, I couldn't even consider myself her husband. It didn't matter how badly I wanted to go after Pishard. I belonged there, with her. There would be a time for revenge, but it wasn't now.

Tanja drifted off to sleep and I settled into the chair next to her.

An hour later, the sheriff called to let us know that he'd questioned James Pishard. "We found him at the pool hall in Santa Rosa, drunk as a skunk," he said. "Said he had been there all night, and he had a dozen witnesses to prove it. He's not our shooter. The bartender asked if I could lock him up anyway."

"Did you?"

"Consider it a late Christmas present."

I hung up laughing, but somewhat disappointed. I was sure the shooter had been Pishard. I fell asleep trying to figure out who else it could have been.

The next morning, I woke with a dull throbbing head-ache and a deep pain in my hip. At some point during the night, a nurse had offered to let me sleep in an adjacent room with an empty bed, but I had refused. I was going to pay for that decision all day long.

Tanja and I shared some sort of rubber-flavored pancakes for breakfast, and before we left, the nurse kindly gave us a handful of the hospital's ten-dollar aspirins. Not long after that, Diekmann and Grandma picked us up.

One of the nurses wheeled Tanja to the front door in a wheelchair, and Diekmann pulled up driving Grandma's old green Malibu. It was strange to see Diekmann sitting where Grandpa had always been. Stranger still, seeing Grandma sitting across the bench seat with that adoring smile as we drove home. I was getting used to it, though. It was nice to see Grandma smiling.

When we pulled up to our house, Tanja gasped. "You fixed the window! How did you find a repairman in the middle of the night?"

"Being the sheriff has certain advantages," Diekmann said with a wink. "Come on, let's get you inside."

I helped Tanja back into the house, but she really didn't need any assistance. The pain in her belly was mostly gone, and as long as she didn't do anything strenuous, it didn't seem to bother her. I, on the other hand, felt bolts of lightning go shooting through my hip every time I moved my left leg.

On the front porch, we found a gift basket from one of our neighbors. It had a bottle of wine, a box of crackers, and several varieties of cheese.

"They must have felt guilty," Diekmann said. "We got seven phone calls last night asking if you were drug dealers."

"What are neighbors for?" Tanja said with a laugh. "I suppose by the end of the week, we'll all be mafia kingpins or serial killers."

"At least they won't be asking to borrow the lawn-mower," I said. I opened the front door and a buzzer went off. I froze.

"Relax, that's your new alarm system," said Diekmann. "Come inside, I'll show you how it works."

Tanja and I didn't know what to say. The sheriff had installed a full-featured alarm system with a key-pad by the front door, and sensors on all the doors and windows. "When the alarm goes off, the system will automatically dial dispatch," he said. "If that happens, just take cover until we get here."

Tanja threw her arms around him. "Thanks, sher-iff."

"Just doing my job, ma'am," he said, doing his best John Wayne impression. As they separated, Grandma stepped closer and put her arm around his waist.

"If the two of you need anything else, you just let us know," she said.

Tanja was on the verge of tears. "I need a shower," she said in a cracking voice. "And some time to pull myself together."

"Take all the time you need, dear. Joe and I will get lunch started."

While Tanja showered, I fired up the barbecue and Grandma threw together a salad. We hadn't been shopping in a while, but I found some ground beef in the freezer. I defrosted the meat and made it into patties. Unfortunately, we didn't have buns, so we were stuck with burgers on white bread. Sometimes, you just have to improvise.

We enjoyed a nice quiet lunch and a few games of cards. At four o'clock, Grandma and Diekmann decided that it was time to give us some privacy. We didn't discuss work or the shooting during the entire afternoon.

After they left, Tanja spent most of the evening in the back bedroom. She said she felt uncomfortable in the living room after what had happened. "It's too easy," she said at one point. "Someone can just walk right up and start shooting. We need to put up a concrete fence, or some bulletproof glass."

"Bulletproof glass the size of our living room window?" I said. "If we had that kind of money, we'd be living in a mansion."

"What can we do, Joe? I feel like a sitting duck."

"A sitting duck with one of the best views in town. You live across the street from a park and a redwood grove. Do you really want to give that up, just because of one lunatic?"

"I don't know. I'm just scared. I'm worried about our baby."

"I know," I said, settling down on the bed next to her. "Look, we both knew this business could be dangerous. If you want me to find something else, just say the word. I hear the construction business is picking up."

"No. Absolutely not. We're going to see this through. This is what we were meant to do. I can feel it."

"Then don't let one bad guy ruin it. He had his shot, and he missed. Now we're on high alert. We have an alarm. He's not coming back here."

"But he's still out there, Joe. He's out there somewhere, just waiting for the chance to try again. Maybe next time he'll get lucky."

"He won't. I promise you that."

Tanja gave me a big hug. "I suppose it's for the best, this happening now. It allows us to work through our feelings."

"Sure it does," I said. I had the sinking feeling all husbands get when they sense a long, emotional conversation bearing down on them.

"It's just frightening, you know? The idea that someone might be out there stalking us."

"It's not just some random stranger," I said. "Somehow, this is connected to the case. Whoever shot at me last night was probably the killer."

Tanja bolted upright in bed, with her eyes open wide. "My things!" she said. "Where are my things?"

"What are you talking about?"

"The bag! The hospital bag with my things in it..."

"Oh."

I stepped around the end of the bed and picked it up. Tanja lunged forward, snatching it out of my hands. She began fighting the zipper, trying to tear it open. Frustrated, she reached out and stole the knife poking out of my jeans pocket. I watched in amazement as Tanja whipped out the blade, slit the bag open across the top, and yanked out Becky's .mp3 player.

"What are you doing?" I said, watching her fumble with the headphones.

"Joe, Becky talked to the killer! *She talked to him!* That's not all. You have to listen to this!" Before I knew it, she was out of bed and wrestling with the headphones. She tried to jam them into my ears, but I pulled away.

"Slow down," I said. "Give me that thing for a second."

I took the .mp3 player from her and walked over to the stereo. I located an adapter cable in the top drawer, and plugged it into the auxiliary input on the stereo. I pressed play, and Becky's voice came drifting out of the speakers.

"Skip past all this," Tanja said, rushing to my side. "Here, give it to me." She ripped the recorder out of my hands and began scanning ahead through the files. At last, she came to the one she was looking for. We listened to it together, staring into one another's eyes as the killer's voice drifted out of the speakers.

"You keep talking like that, you're gonna end up just like them," he said.

"Just like them," Tanja repeated. "He killed that missing boy, Joe. He murdered Myles Meyer, and Becky's father." She skipped back, and played the whole recording a second time.

"They never found Meyer's body," I said. "If he was murdered, his body is still out there somewhere."

"That's it, Joe!"

"What are you talking about?"

She settled onto the edge of the bed, staring at me with a wondrous gaze. "That's why Becky and Randall were at the reservoir. They were trying to find Myles Meyer's body. Think about it: why else would they be there? They didn't meet at that secluded spot to have an affair. They met because Becky convinced Randall to help her. She knew something, something that would prove her father had been murdered. That was the big story Randall was talking about. He was going to expose a double murder!"

"That's why she had a shovel and pickaxe in the trunk of her car," I said.

"Yes, exactly! Meyer's body must be buried up there somewhere."

I started pulling on my boots as we were talking. I didn't even realize what I was doing until Tanja said, "Joe, what are you doing?"

"Um... getting dressed?"

"No, you're not. It's almost bedtime. It can wait until tomorrow. Besides, we're going to need help to find that body."

I glanced out the bedroom window and realized it had been dark for three hours. It was starting to rain again. No wonder my leg was so stiff. I pulled my boots off and limped to the bathroom in search of an aspirin.

"Joe," Tanja said in a quiet voice. "Do you think he's killed anybody else?"

"No," I said. I turned off the light and crawled into bed with her.

"How can you be sure?"

"Because I'm tired. Too tired for this case to become any more complicated tonight."

She giggled and pulled the covers up to her chin. "I love you, Joe."

"Wear your seatbelt," I said with a smile.

She snuggled up against me.

The seatbelt thing is sort of an old joke between the two of us. At one point, after we had been dating a

136

while, Tanja made a big deal out of the fact that I'd never said I loved her. Of course, she knew that I was no good at things like that. I don't like talking about my feelings. I don't like *sharing*. It's not that I don't feel emotions; I just don't wear them on my sleeve.

Of course, It didn't make matters any easier that Tanja had put me on the spot. You can't just tell a guy that he should say he loves you. It doesn't work that way. Of course, I had just assumed that she *knew* I loved her. Why else would I have been dating her and spending all that time and money on her? Wasn't it obvious? Why do women always have to make things so complicated?

At any rate, after our date, Tanja was getting into her car to go home for the night. I told her to put on her seatbelt. She smiled and said:

"So you do love me."

I smiled and leaned into the window to kiss her. Of course, Tanja had known all along how I felt about her. She was an FBI agent with years of training on body language and psychology. She had just been giving me a hard time. Ever since, I've returned the favor by telling her to wear a seatbelt instead of saying that I love her. It has been a running joke between us for as long as we've been together.

With our new alarm system installed and a loaded forty-five under my pillow, I slept like a baby. It was the first sound sleep I'd had in three days. Tanja hadn't turned on the alarm clock, so we both ended up sleeping in. She woke me at nine a.m.

"At least we're not late for work," I said cheerfully as I headed for the shower. My hip was feeling much better, and that instantly put me in a good mood.

"That's the nice thing about being self-employed," I said. "It's like every day is Saturday."

"It's also like every day is *never* Saturday," Tanja said as she joined me in the shower. "These days when we get a day off, it's a bad thing. It means we're not making any money."

"You have a point. They say that when you start a business, you have to ask yourself: *Is it better to work forty hours for someone else, or eighty for yourself?*"

"What's your answer?"

"I'm not sure, but I bet most self-employed people wouldn't change for the world."

The soap fell on the floor, and we stared at each other.

"Well, pick it up," she said.

I raised an eyebrow. "You first."

"Not a chance."

"It's a standoff," I said, narrowing my eyes. Tanja pulled me close, and put her arms around my neck.

"Let's just stand here for a while."

After we had the soap issue worked out, I left Tanja in the shower while I toweled off and got dressed. I called Diekmann to tell him about the recording, and our theory about the killer.

"We think Meyer's body might be around that reservoir somewhere," I said.

"That would explain the shovel in Becky's trunk. There isn't much I can do to help, but I can call Santa Rosa P.D., and ask them to send over a K-9 unit. They have a shepherd that's trained for that sort of thing."

"That's a long shot, isn't it?" I said. "If there really is a body around that lake, it has been buried there almost twenty-five years."

138

"I'm no expert," he said. "I'll ask what they think. I suppose a metal detector wouldn't hurt, if you can get your hands on one."

I thanked him and hung up. Tanja saw me frowning as she came out of the shower. She asked what was wrong, and I explained the situation.

"How much do metal detectors cost?" she said.

"Too much. If the dogs don't work out, I'll call around and see if I can find a rental."

The doorbell rang, and I tensed up. I pulled my gun out from under my pillow and tucked it into the back of my jeans. Tanja started getting dressed as I went down the hall to take a peek out the kitchen window. I saw a delivery van parked out front. I opened the door and a tall, thin guy in a brown shirt asked me to sign for a certified letter. As he drove away, I opened it and scanned the first paragraph.

"What do you have there?" Tanja said in the hallway behind me.

"It's a foreclosure notice. Says if we don't make a payment in forty-eight hours, they'll start proceedings."

"Joe, we have to cash that check. We can't put it off any longer. We can't risk losing our home."

I handed her the letter. "Do it," I said. "It'll buy us some time. Hopefully, we'll be able to pay Grandma back soon."

"I don't think Grandma expects us to pay her back."

"It doesn't matter. We're going to anyway."

Tanja accepted that quietly. She retrieved the check from the bedroom. She also came out with her small gun safe, the one she keeps locked up in the back of the closet.

"What are you doing?" I said.

She opened the box and pulled out her little 9mm Glock and a pair of earplugs. "Just playing it safe," she said. "Until we catch that psycho, I'm not taking any chances."

"Earplugs?" I said. "What are you going to do, ask the maniac to wait a few seconds while you put in your earplugs?"

"Very funny." She tucked the gun and earplugs into her purse and held up Grandma's check. "You ready?"

Fifteen minutes later, Tanja had already deposited the check into our account at the Vine Hill Credit Union. She made an instant payment to our mortgage online, using her cell phone. The whole process took about two minutes.

"It's done," she said with a sigh of relief.

"That fast?"

"They make it very easy to give them money."

"Somehow I doubt it would be so simple if *they* owed *us*," I grumbled.

"I know you don't like taking money Joe, but it was the right thing to do. We can pay Grandma back. We can make payments."

I glanced at the clock. "Diekmann called. He said the K-9 unit will be at the reservoir in less than an hour."

"Perfect, let's go!"

I don't know why, but for some reason when Diekmann had said a K-9 unit was coming, I assumed half a dozen city cops and a team of highly trained dogs would meet us. I was a bit surprised when an old Blazer appeared at the top of hill. As we parked, a gray haired woman in her fifties climbed out. She introduced herself as

140

Marge. She opened the tailgate, releasing a German shepherd and two collies.

She must have noted my look, because she said, "Don't let them fool you. Last winter they found a skier buried under twenty feet of ice in Tahoe."

"Oh my God," said Tanja. "Did he survive?"

Marge wrinkled up her forehead. "No. He was buried under twenty feet of ice. He had been there for two years."

"What should we do?" I said.

"Just stand back, and try not to distract the dogs. We'll walk around the area a few times. When they stop and sit, that's what we call a *hit*. That means they smell something they've been trained to find. Maybe a body, maybe not. If they do that, I'll put down a small flag and we will come back to the spot again in a little while."

Tanja and I stayed out of the way as Marge gave the dogs a search command, and they went to work. As we watched, the group covered the circumference of the lake and the surrounding area three times. The first time around, they hit on seven different spots. Marge later explained that some of these were probably places where animals had been buried, or had died over the years. She told us to be patient.

During that time, Diekmann arrived. Tanja had crawled into the passenger seat in the Suburban because her back was starting to hurt. Diekmann and I stood next to her so we could talk quietly while we waited.

"I brought a few shovels and a pickaxe," he said. "Unfortunately, there was a shooting up Chalk Hill and I can't spare any men. It's just you and me, Joe. How's your leg?"

"I'll be okay," I said. I wasn't about to tell him that it had been aching for two days, ever since I first jumped into that lake. I wasn't going to let a little pain stop me.

"Good. We'll see how far we get. If it gets too rough, we'll rent a Bobcat."

I laughed, and then realized he was serious.

"A tractor?" I said. "Won't that damage evidence?"

"Probably," said Diekmann. "But not much more than burying it for twenty-five years."

On their last trip around the lake, the canines zeroed in on two spots, one at the southern end of the reservoir near the road, the other just beyond the bushes, a few yards from the collapsed dock.

"I pulled all the flags except those two," Marge said as she loaded up her dogs. "If you find anything, it'll be in one of those two spots."

We thanked her for her help, and Marge went on her way. Diekmann and I decided to start with the one closest to the road. We grabbed our shovels and went to work.

Thankfully, several months of persistent rain had saturated the ground, so the digging was easy. Even with my bum leg, I managed to hold up my end of the work. Fifteen minutes in, we found a bone. Diekmann examined it and proclaimed that we had discovered the corpse of a murdered cow.

I told him Tanja and I would accept a cashier's check for payment. He said the check was in the mail. We moved on.

The second likely spot was a bit harder to work. The soil was rocky and tangled with the roots of the nearby shrubs. We encountered several large stones that consumed a great deal of time and energy to remove, and left both of us panting and dripping with sweat. By then, it was getting dark and my leg was starting to hurt pretty bad. I kept that to myself.

Tanja took the Suburban back to town to pick up some dinner and flashlights. By the time she returned, full night had fallen, and she found the two of us resting at the edge of the hill, talking about the old days. We had no place to eat, so the three of us crawled into the Suburban to enjoy our greasy dinner of cheeseburgers and stale fries. It was a less than spectacular end to a long, hard afternoon. It started to rain while we were eating.

When he was finished, Diekmann reached around to put his trash in one of the bags and groaned as his back muscles seized up. He froze with a look of pure anguish.

"You going to be all right?" I said.

"Just... breathing..." he whispered. "Give me a minute. Or three."

"I think you need to call it a day," Tanja said. "We can come back tomorrow."

"Not me," said Diekmann. "I've got a meeting with the city council in the morning."

"Wait here and let your back unwind," I said. " I want to get that last rock out before I give up."

Diekmann protested, but only halfheartedly. He knew when he was beat. I threw on one of the ponchos Tanja had brought back with her, and went stumbling back to the hole with a gas lantern and an old shovel. The rain had picked up steadily while we were eating, and a pool of water had begun to form in the bottom of the hole.

I threw my back into my work, using my weight against the shovel's handle as a lever to pry the rock upward. I ignored the pain in my hip, steadily working at the stone until I finally heard the sucking sound I was looking for. As the rock began to move, mud and water rushed in to fill the gap. I reached the end of my leverage, and the rock fell back into place. I was close, but it wasn't ready to come out yet.

I moved to the other side of the hole and tried again. I jammed the tip of the shovel under the corner and stomped on it a few times to make sure I had a good bite. I leaned on the handle, pressing down with all my weight. All at once, the rock moved and the handle snapped. Before I knew what had happened, I was sprawled out face down in the mud with excruciating jolts of pain shooting up and down my leg.

I cried out, blinded by pain, twisting around as I tried to get my face out of the mud. I got an arm underneath my chest, giving me some room to breathe, and then went still, moaning quietly as I waiting for the agony to subside.

For some reason, when my bones healed after that old injury, they ended up slightly out of whack. I've already explained that once in a while my leg decides to give out on me. When the stars align just right, and I put too much weight on it at just the wrong time, my hip tries to twist out of the socket. When it does, it's about the most god-awful pain imaginable. It pinches a nerve that nearly cripples me. The doctors say I'll probably need a new hip someday, but I have this philosophy about trying to keep my original body parts intact as long as I can.

This has only happened to me a few times. Every time it does, I have a good reminder to be very careful with that leg for a year or so. Then I forget. I get careless.

This time, the pain was bad enough at first that I completely lost any sense of who or where I was. After what was probably just one minute, but seemed more like a day and a half, I heard footsteps sloshing through the mud in my direction. The pain hadn't abated much, but shock must have been kicking in because I started to come around. I felt Tanja's hands on my shoulders as she bent over and tried to lift me. I waved her away.

"Don't!" I said. "Just give me a minute." She stood back, and I looked her up and down, rolling my eyes. "Are you crazy, woman? Get back in the car! You're going to catch pneumonia."

"I'm not the idiot lying in the mud," she curtly replied. I didn't bother reminding her that she was pregnant. I figured she knew. I heard a snort, and swiveled my head around to see Diekmann staring down into the hole.

"What?" I said.

He looked at me and shook his head. "You enjoy making me work in the rain, son?"

"Huh?"

He stepped into the hole, bent down, and held something up. Tanja lifted the lantern so we could clearly see the object. It was a human skull.

"You've done it now," Diekmann said. "I'm gonna be here all damn night."

Chapter 11

Tanja

Over the next two hours, a steady stream of police personnel joined us at the reservoir. The Sheriff's men helped Joe get into the Suburban, but Joe insisted we stick around, even though he was in excruciating pain.

"Just a while," he said. "I want to make sure it's the right body."

I gave him a concerned look. "Joe, if we've found another body and it isn't Myles, we must be sitting on an ancient burial ground."

Joe didn't quite get my joke. I think he was in too much pain to understand me. He took a Tylenol and crawled into the backseat.

It was after ten p.m. when the sheriff finally came over and announced that we had officially discovered the remains of a pubescent male.

"We'll move the remains to the morgue for testing and identification," he said. "The rest of the excavation will have to wait until morning. Go get some rest, Joe."

"Do you think you'll find anything else?" I said.

"I didn't think we'd find this," said the sheriff. "Go home."

I didn't argue. I took Joe home and tucked him into bed with a nice hot buttered rum. A little while later, he called for a second. I noticed that his color was coming back. That was the last I heard from him. I went to bed half an hour later and he was snoring like a freight train.

When I woke the next morning, Joe was still out of it. I left a bottle of aspirin and a glass of water on the nightstand next to the bed, and went to make some breakfast. Unfortunately, we were down to pickles, toast, and prenatal vitamins. Try as I might, I couldn't come up with a clever breakfast idea based on those ingredients.

I made a quick trip to the supermarket. When I got back, I found Joe lying awake in bed. I noticed that the glass of water was empty and the aspirin bottle was sitting open.

"You okay?" I said.

"Just waiting. I think the third pill just kicked in."

"Joe! How many did you take?"

"How many? I'm not done yet."

"Yes, you are." I took the aspirin back to the bathroom and brought him a cup of coffee. "Drink that, and then get moving before that hip freezes up on you."

Joe moaned and grunted a lot, but he stumbled into the shower without too much argument. Twenty minutes later, he wandered into the kitchen leaning heavily on his cane. I set a plate of pancakes and bacon on the counter, and refilled his coffee cup.

"Where'd all this food come from?" he said.

"I went to the store."

He stared at me, mystified. "What time is it?"

"Ten thirty." Joe blinked. He didn't say anything; he just went to work on the food. By the time the plate was empty, he was acting half-human again, and even talking like one.

"Have you heard from Diekmann?"

"He had that meeting this morning. I'm hoping he'll update us by afternoon."

"What do we do in the meanwhile?"

"I want to visit the high school again."

"For what?"

"I've been thinking. If that body we found last night really was Myles Meyer, there must be a connection between him and Richard Sweet. The killer must be someone they both knew."

"And he's at the high school?" Joe said, looking askance.

"No, moron. Remember the pictures in Becky's notebook? Richard Sweet and Myles Meyer went to school together. I want to see their records."

"Ah."

Joe refilled his plate and picked at it for a while. I could tell he wasn't eager to get back on his feet, but I eventually told him it was time to get moving. He resigned himself to his fate with a loud sigh, and we headed for the door.

Half an hour later, we were back at Healdsburg High School. Linda, the freckle-faced woman at the front desk, greeted us with an irritated sigh.

"Back again so soon?" she said.

"Yes, I would like to view some students' records from nineteen-ninety."

She sighed again. "That's not our policy. Would you like to speak with the principal?"

"Yes, please."

I turned to Joe and found him grinning.

"What's so funny?" I said quietly.

"I don't think she likes us much."

"I don't think she likes *anyone* who makes her get her lazy butt out of that chair."

Joe laughed. "She is kind of sexy, though. In a hostile, apathetic sort of way."

I punched him in the shoulder. Linda returned a few minutes later with a very short, very bald man with a mustache.

"I'm Chester Balfour," he said. "Linda tells me you're looking for old records?"

"Yes, from nineteen-ninety. We want to cross reference your records for Richard Sweet and Myles Meyer."

"Do you have a warrant?"

"Do we need one?" said Joe. "We are talking about two murder victims."

"Rules are rules," he said. "I can't let one person break the rules, or everyone will want to."

"Mr. Balfour," I said. "We're not children. We're investigators trying to solve a murder. What can it hurt to see those records?"

"I've done all I can," he said dismissively, and disappeared back inside his office. Joe and I stared at each other, dumbfounded.

"Better luck next time," said Linda with a snarky grin.

"Count on it," I said. "Next time, we'll have a warrant. And we'll be asking to see a lot more than two files."

Her eyebrows went up.

"Yep," Joe said. "That's going to be a huge mess. I've seen these guys serve a warrant before. Everything ends up in one big pile on the floor. It can take weeks to sort it out after they're finished."

"I know I'd hate to be the one in charge of putting it all back together," I said.

Linda gulped. "You know, I just had a thought. You might want to try the school library. That's where we keep the old yearbooks. I don't know if that's any help or not."

"Thanks," I said. "We'll take a look."

We left the office and walked down the hall. Joe was leaning heavily on his cane, and I couldn't help feeling sorry for him, but he was grinning from ear to ear.

"You handled that pretty well," he said. "I think Linda was about to have a panic attack."

"It didn't do much good."

"She told us about the yearbooks, didn't she?"

I rolled my eyes. "We didn't come here to look at yearbooks, Joe. I want to see those files."

"I'll come back later," he said.

"Later?"

"Yes, after dark. After everyone goes home."

I lowered my voice. "Joe, are you talking about breaking and entering?"

"Of course not. I don't plan on breaking anything."

I stopped, and turned to face him. "Breaking and entering is not subjective," I said quietly. "It's against the law. As someone who used to be a police officer, I think you would appreciate that."

"Pfft. When I was undercover, breaking and entering was part of my job description. Besides, it's not like I haven't busted into this place before..."

"Joe!"

"Relax, Fed. I'm just kidding. Although technically, as private citizens, we have a lot more leeway in this sort of thing."

"That doesn't matter. We have to do the right thing."

"Which in this case, means finding the killer."

"Don't drag me into something like this, Joe."

"What are you talking about? I told you I would come alone."

"That's the problem. I have to go with you, because you'll probably fall down, break your hip, and be stuck here all night like a ninety-year-old man. Unless you die of a blood clot or something. Wouldn't that make a nice story for our baby?"

"Geez, forget I said anything." He went hobbling down the hallway and I stared after him a minute. A slight smile came to my lips. I'm getting him trained, but this sort of thing takes time.

Joe turned the corner and disappeared, and I hurried after him. By the time I caught up to him, he was already thanking the school librarian.

Joe motioned for me to follow him, and he led the way to the back wall. There, we found a collection of yearbooks going back to 1964. Joe pulled out the 1990 edition, and we settled down at one of the tables to thumb through the pages.

"Joe and Myles were both students at the same time," Joe confirmed, pointing out their pictures. "Let's check the sports section. They may have played football together, or baseball."

We flipped through the pages and found nothing. We checked the other extracurricular activities and clubs, and found neither Richard nor Myles in any of them. I was about to give up when Joe flipped the page again, and landed on the Journalism spread. I gasped.

I was staring at a photo of Myles Meyer, Richard Sweet, and James Pishard. They were posing with a mockup of the yearbook I was holding. A much younger Mr. King was standing behind the three boys, smiling.

Joe looked at me. "Are you thinking what I'm thinking?"

"That it's awfully strange that Solomon King never mentioned his relationship with Becky's father?" I said.

"Uh-huh."

"Perhaps he didn't think it was relevant. You remember what Kendra said. Everybody in this town knows everybody else."

"Look at the picture again," Joe said. "I see four people there, and half of them have been murdered."

I stared at him. "You're saying one of the others is the killer. Either Solomon King, or James Pishard?"

Joe leaned back in his seat. "I don't know, but what are the odds? There's a connection there. More than the obvious fact that they were King's students."

"I think we need to have another talk with Solomon" I said.

"Perfect," said Joe. "I know where he works. As I recall, it's about a hundred yards from here."

Just as we arrived, the bell rang and hundreds of students filed into the halls. As the journalism classroom emptied, Joe and I stepped inside. Solomon King was at the far end of the room, looking over a student's shoulder, discussing something in his notebook. Joe cleared his throat, and Mr. King practically jumped out of his skin.

"Oh!" he said, blinking at us. "You surprised me."

"Do you have a few minutes?" I said.

"Not really. I have a meeting in the teachers' lounge..."

"It'll just take a minute," said Joe.

"I suppose so. Alec, we'll work on this assignment later."

The boy closed his binder, shoved it into his back-pack, and left quietly. Mr. King came over to us. "So what's this about? Have you learned anything about that poor girl who was killed?"

"Yes, we have," Joe said with a smile. I opened up the yearbook and pointed out the image we'd found.

"Is that you, Mr. King?" I said.

"Yes, of course. Why?"

"You didn't tell us that these three boys were in your class."

"I don't understand. Why is that important?"

"Can you tell us where you were on the night Becky Sweet was killed?" said Joe.

King's gaze danced between us. "I don't under-stand... are you accusing me of killing that poor girl?"

"Just answer the question," said Joe.

"I can't. That was five years ago. I have no idea. I might be able to go through my old calendars, but-"

"What about Myles Meyer?" I said, cutting him off. "Where were you when he was murdered?"

Mr. King's face paled. "I... I'm not sure..."

"It was 1990," said Joe. "I'm sure you remember. It happened right after this picture was taken."

Mr. King looked faint. "I need to sit down," he said. He walked around us and settled into his chair. He began to massage his forehead.

"Do we need to call the sheriff?" I said.

"No, please. Just give me a moment." He leaned back, crossing his arms. "I was always afraid this would happen. All these years... I was always afraid it would come to this."

"To what?" said Joe. "Did you think you'd never get caught?"

"No, you don't understand. Please, have a seat. I will explain everything."

Joe and I pulled two chairs up to his desk.

"You're right, of course," he said. "I knew those boys. I knew them all very well. The truth is, I was something of a father figure to them. You see, they were latchkey kids. Generation X; the first generation of kids to go home after school to an empty house." He leaned back, crossing one leg over the other as he summoned the memory.

"All three boys had absentee parents, or parents that were neglectful, possibly even abusive. In my job, you see signs, but you never can be sure. I try to watch out for them, I really do." He shifted as he spoke, right to left and back again, as if he couldn't get comfortable.

"What happened?" I said.

"The boys used to party a lot. They liked to drink, smoke some marijuana... they were just being boys, really. I knew what they were doing, but I didn't say anything. I thought it was better for them to blow off some steam that way, rather than picking fights or vandalizing property. For kids like that, with so much anger and energy, it has to go somewhere. They need an outlet."

"So you *gave them* drugs and alcohol?" said Joe.

"No! Of course not. I just heard things. Heard them planning things, here and there. Instead of saying something, I just smiled knowingly. What was I supposed to do? I never thought it would come to any harm."

"What does all of this have to do with Myles' death?" said Joe.

King leaned forward, putting his head in his hands. "The children used to go to a lake near Vine Hill. A place just off the road."

"The reservoir?" said Joe. "At the dairy farm?"

"Yes, that's the place. The teenagers used to gather there, because it was private. It was close to town, but far enough out of town that they wouldn't be caught drinking. I don't think the old farmer paid much attention to what was going on there. It was across the road from the dairy, and out of sight."

"That's the same place where Becky was killed," I said. "Why didn't you tell us this before?"

"Because I was afraid," he said.

"Afraid of what?" said Joe. "Prison?"

"No. I told you, it's not like that. I didn't kill Myles. But I might know who did."

"Who?" said Joe.

He sighed. "One day, Myles didn't show up for school. I didn't think much of it at first, but then he was absent the next day, and the next. Of course, by then his disappearance was all over the news. I could tell by watching Richard and James that they both knew something. They had been acting strange all week. I asked them to stay after class, and that's when they told me what had happened."

"Go on," I said.

"The boys told me they had been out drinking, and that Myles had fallen and hit his head on a rock. It killed him instantly. Naturally, they were terrified. They all had drugs and alcohol in their systems, and they had been trespassing on private property. They were afraid the police would accuse them of murder, and they had no way to prove it was an accident. So instead of coming forward, they hid the body."

155

"And you kept this secret?" I said. "Mr. King, that's obstruction of justice. What were you thinking?"

"I was thinking of them!" he said. "Don't you see what it would have done to them? Their lives were already hard enough. Lousy or nonexistent parents, reputations for getting into trouble. The police would have come down hard on those boys. They would have made the boys into examples. And for what? None of that would bring Myles back."

"What about his parents?" said Joe. "Do you have any idea how they must have suffered all these years?"

"Would they have suffered less, after sending two innocent boys to prison?"

"What about Becky?" I said. "How is her death connected to this?"

"She came to me before she died. She was researching her father's death. She believed he had been murdered. I believe James Pishard must have learned about this, and decided to stop her before she found out what had really happened to Myles."

A silence fell over the room as we considered that possibility.

"Hold on," said Joe. "You're saying that James killed both Becky, and her father? All to cover up an accidental death?"

"I don't know how else to explain it," said King. "Perhaps James feared Richard would go to the police. He may have killed Richard to keep him quiet. A few years later, Becky started asking questions."

"If that's true, you must have suspected it," I said. "Why didn't you come forward before now?"

"I was afraid!" he said. "Don't you understand that? Because if I was right about Richard, if James was willing to kill Becky, too, then he would surely kill me."

"Do you realize that you could be considered an accessory to murder?" I said.

Mr. King closed his eyes and began massaging his temples. "I knew what would happen to me if I came forward, so I kept my mouth shut. I stayed alive. That's all."

Joe leaned forward. "Mr. King, has it occurred to you that Myles' death may not have been *an accident?*"

"Of course it has. Looking back now, it makes perfect sense. Back then, I was just trying to help those boys."

"You may have helped them get away with murder," I said.

"I'm sorry. I didn't mean for any of this to happen. I was just trying to protect those poor children, and later, I was afraid..."

"Will you testify to all of this in court?" I said.

King leaned forward, resting his elbows on his desk. "Only in exchange for immunity."

"We need to call the sheriff," Joe said. "Mr. King, don't leave town."

On the way back to the Suburban, I told Joe that Mr. King had been lying to us. He stopped, and turned to stare at me.

"Lying about what?"

"I don't know. All I can be sure of is the fact that he was hiding something from us. And when he was thinking about what had happened, he kept looking to the left."

"What does that mean?"

"It means he wasn't searching for memories, he was *creating* them. He was using his imagination instead of his recall."

"Are you sure?"

"Not one hundred percent. I know the signs, but I can't guarantee their accuracy. You know that."

"Maybe he was just nervous," said Joe. "He had good reason to be, all things considered."

"Or perhaps he was just covering."

"Covering for what?"

"I don't know."

Joe and I hurried back to the car, and I called Sheriff Diekmann as soon as we were on the road. I explained the situation. After hanging up, I turned to Joe.

"Diekmann is going to issue a warrant for Pishard. He said they should have him in custody within the hour." Joe grinned from ear to ear.

"Let's go wait at the department. I want to see that piece of trash do the perp walk."

"Joe... I've gotta eat, honey."

"Drive-thru?"

I sighed. "It's a good thing I take prenatal vitamins. Promise me we'll start eating real food as soon as this case is over."

"Scout's honor. Don't worry, it won't be long now. I can feel it."

We swung through the drive-thru on our way out of town, and hurried back to the sheriff's department. Half an hour later, Joe and I were in the break room finishing our lunch when they brought Pishard in.

We heard the commotion outside and rushed to the door to see two deputies ushering him through the front door. He was not happy. Pishard had already spent the night locked up on a drunk and disorderly charge, and was back in custody less than eight hours later. He also still had a nice purple glow around his eye from Joe's right hook three days earlier.

There was a lot of screaming about lawyers and lawsuits, about abuse of power and so on. Things finally got quiet when they shoved him into an interrogation room and cuffed him to the chair. A few seconds later, Diekmann appeared in the doorway of the break room.

"Pishard has agreed to an interview without his lawyer," Diekmann said with a grin. "Seems they had a falling out after our last talk. You two ready?"

"You're letting us go in?" said Joe.

"I can't think of anyone more deserving," he said. "Or motivated. Just don't hit him, Joe. Think you can manage that?"

Joe blinked his eyes innocently. Diekmann snorted and shook his head.

"Do you mind if I ask the questions?" I said.

"I don't see why not. You're the one with all the fancy-pants training."

Pishard was sitting behind a small metal table with his hands cuffed behind his back when the three of us walked in. He was furious, and instantly went into a tirade.

"I'm going to sue you for false arrest!" he shouted, staring at Diekmann. "This is harassment."

"You can't sue me for false arrest, because you haven't been charged yet," said Diekmann. "Besides, you don't have a lawyer anymore, remember?"

"Then what am I doing here? Why am I handcuffed to this chair?"

"We've taken you into custody. I can hold you for forty-eight hours if I want, so I suggest you try to cooperate. We just want to ask you a few questions."

Joe settled down across from him. Diekmann and I both remained standing. I looked Pishard up and down, trying to gauge his emotions. I turned to sheriff.

"Can you take off his cuffs?" I said.

Diekmann raised his eyebrows. "You sure you want to do that?"

"He's not going anywhere," Joe said, cracking his knuckles. Pishard threw his gaze back and forth between the three of us, trying to figure out what was going on.

"This some kind of mind game?" he said. "Like a good-cop, bad-cop thing?"

Diekmann sighed and stepped around the table to remove the cuffs. "I hope you know what you're doing," he said.

Pishard massaged his wrists and propped his elbows up on the table.

"Better?" I said. Pishard shot me a sarcastic grin. Joe leaned closer, and he shifted nervously.

"Where were you last night?" I said.

"At the pool hall. The sheriff already knows that. That's where he arrested me for no reason."

"Drunk and disorderly was the charge, I believe," said Diekmann.

"You were just looking for an excuse."

"I did drop the charges, James. Don't make me regret that."

I watched Pishard's body language as he spoke. James sat leaning slightly to the right, with both arms on the table, his legs open. He looked reasonably comfortable. Pishard's demeanor and lack of movement implied that he was telling the truth. But I already knew that. I just needed a baseline of behavior to determine whether his body language would be reliable.

"Did you kill Becky Sweet?" I said abruptly.

He fixed his gaze on me, but otherwise remained motionless. "I thought you had decided my worthless kid killed her."

"Did you kill her or not?" I said, pressing him.

"No."

I was looking for a signal, a movement that would indicate his guilt, or at least his discomfort with the subject. A hand over his face, or arms crossing over his chest perhaps. I saw none of that.

"What about Myles Meyer?"

Pishard's eyes widened. He leaned back in the chair, crossing his legs first, and then crossing his arms over his chest. *Bingo.*

"I don't know what you're talking about."

"Yes, you do. You went to school with him. You were friends. Would you like to see the yearbook pictures?"

He shook his head. He leaned forward and fixed his gaze on the table.

"What aren't you telling us, Pishard?"

"Nothing."

"You understand we have evidence?" I said. "Meyer had several well preserved items in his coat. A marijuana pipe, for example, and a bottle of booze. We're searching for fingerprints and D.N.A. evidence right now."

Pishard looked at me uncertainly, then turned his gaze on Diekmann and Joe. He straightened himself. "Then you'll know it wasn't me, pretty soon," he said.

"If it wasn't you, who was it?"

"Mr. King, of course."

Joe snorted. "Come on, we know better than that."

161

"You don't know jack," Pishard said with a smirk. "And whatever that old pervert told you, I guarantee he was jerking you around."

Pishard leaned back in the chair and opened his arms. I tried not to show my surprise.

"That sounds far-fetched," I said. "Would you care to explain?"

He grinned at me. He leaned forward and lowered his voice, as if sharing an important secret: "I didn't actually see it, but I was *there* that day."

"Where?"

"At the lake, where Myles died."

"What happened?" I said.

"Mr. King liked to hang out with us kids a lot. I mean *a lot*. He used to party with us."

"That's a serious accusation," Diekmann said. "Think about what you're saying."

"It's the truth!" Pishard snarled. "The guy was a creep. I mean, we didn't realize it. We all just thought he was cool, you know? He liked to party with the kids. He'd buy us booze and get stoned. How many adults would do that?"

"None that want to stay out of prison," Diekmann said.

"I know that now. Like I said, back then we were just stupid kids."

"Even if it's true, that doesn't prove anything," I said. "I hope you have a better story than that."

I was cautious with my language, trying not to lead him. I wanted him to draw the entire story out of his memory, not out of his imagination. His eyes would tell me which.

"We were at the lake one day," he began. "Out at the dairy farm. I'm sure you know the place. It was just

162

the four of us: Ricky, Myles, Mr. King, and me. Ricky and I decided to go for a swim. Myles stayed behind with Mr. King. A few minutes later, we heard a scream. Ricky and I were all the way out in the middle of the lake, so it took a minute to get back to shore. When we got there, Myles was dead. There was a bloody rock on the ground next to him. Mr. King said Myles had fallen down and hit his head."

"You don't believe him?" I said. "That Myles fell?"

"I did at first, but later I thought about it and remembered a few things. Like the bruise Mr. King had on his cheek, and the way he always used to... we always made a joke of it, but he was very *affectionate*."

I watched him closely for even a flicker of conflicting cues, but there were none. He sat facing me, arms and legs open, eyes dancing occasionally to the right as he sorted through his memories. His body language had been consistent from the moment we met, and as far as I could tell, he was speaking the absolute truth.

"Why didn't you go to the police?" I said.

"Why do you think? We all knew what would happen. Mr. King said we were known as troublemakers, and that when the cops did blood tests and found out what we'd been up to, they would arrest us. He said it would ruin our lives, and the only way out of it was to hide the body so no one would ever know."

Diekmann stepped up to the table and leaned close, looking down at Pishard. "That is a very serious accusation, Mr. Pishard. You realize that if I arrest Solomon King under these charges, it will utterly destroy his life?"

"Good! He deserves it. That dude is a perv."

"And you're willing to testify to all of this, in court?"

"Absolutely."

Chapter 12

Joe

We regrouped in Diekmann's office. Pishard was still in the interrogation room, waiting to be released or booked into custody. Diekmann pulled off his baseball cap and ran a hand through his hair.

"I can't hold him," the sheriff said quietly. "Tanja, your bluff about having evidence was great, but unfortunately, the truth is that we don't have it, and without it, I can't charge him. Do you think he was telling the truth about King?"

"I don't know if he's telling the *entire* truth, but his side of the story makes a lot more sense than King's, and his body language backed up everything he said in there."

"What about King?"

"He was keeping something from Joe and me. All I got from him was mixed signals. I can't say how much of what he told us was the truth, but I'm sure that some of it was not. I'm more inclined to believe Pishard, by a long shot."

"All right, I trust your judgment. As much as I hate to do it, I guess I'll cut Pishard loose and go round up Mr. King. This is going to be one heck of a story."

"He should still be at the school," said Tanja.

Diekmann checked his watch. "I'll wait for the classroom to empty out, and then bring him in. I'd hate to destroy the man's career and find out this was all a mistake. Are you two coming with me?"

"What do you think?" Tanja said.

The high school was a madhouse when we arrived. We had just missed the bell, and cars were streaming through the neighborhood streets like ants on a picnic basket. Tanja and I discussed the case as we made our way through traffic. At last, we pulled through the tall metal gates to the high school campus.

"Seems like we were just here," I said in a sarcastic voice.

"That's because we were. I can't say I'm surprised, though."

"I am. I never would have pegged King as a pedophile, much less as a killer. He seems so... I don't know, distinguished I guess."

"The word pedophile may be a bit extreme in this case," Tanja said. "These are high school kids we're talking about. They're almost adults."

"Grandpa used to have a saying: *Almost only counts in horseshoes and hand grenades.*"

"Yes, but kids that age are already sexually active," Tanja said. "Does it really make a difference if they choose a lover who is seventeen years old instead of eighteen?"

"Legally, it does. Besides, we're not talking about an eighteen year old. We're talking about a teacher who holds power over these kids. Anybody who takes advantage of a situation like that is a scumbag."

"Is everything black and white to you?"

"It is today."

"What about Pishard?"

I frowned at her. "What are you talking about?"

"Admit it, you wanted him to be the killer just because you don't like him."

"That's ridiculous. Pishard's a punk either way, and if he ever comes close to my family again, he'll regret it."

I smiled grimly as I pulled into a parking spot and turned off the ignition. As I parked, I saw two police cruisers coming down the lane behind us.

"Let's go get a bad guy," I said.

We joined Diekmann and his deputies, and then crossed the parking lot and made our way towards King's classroom. When we got there, we found the door locked.

"He's not here," Tanja said. "We'd better check with the front desk."

"I already did," said Diekmann. "I called on the way over here, and they told me he'd be here until five."

Tanja turned to face me with a worried look. "We spooked him, Joe. He's making a run for it."

Diekmann radioed the station and found King's address. He told us to meet him there. It was just across town, so we were all there in five minutes. Between the two squad cars, Diekmann's truck, and our Suburban, it looked like his house was being raided. The entire neighborhood came out to see what was going on.

Unfortunately, there was nothing going on. King's house was dark and empty, and it only took a minute to verify that he was gone.

"He's definitely on the run," Tanja said. "He made a huge mess in the bedroom, packing his things."

"He could be at the airport by now," I said. "Or halfway to the next state."

As we left the house, one of the neighbors watching us caught my eye. It was the skateboarding girl we'd seen outside King's classroom. I approached her.

"Do you know Mr. King?" I said. She nodded, and her bangs fell over her eyes. She swiped them away with her left hand, and I caught a glimpse of a tattoo.

"You just missed him," she said. "He came by the house about an hour ago, and then took off in a hurry."

"Did he say anything about where he was going?" Tanja said.

"No."

"How about luggage?" I asked. "Did he have a suitcase or duffel bag with him?"

"Yes, he had a bag. The strange thing was that I waved at him as he was leaving, but he ignored me. Mr. King is usually really friendly, but this time he looked right at me and didn't even say 'Hi' or anything. It was like he looked right through me."

"Thanks," Tanja said.

Diekmann walked up to us wearing rubber gloves and carrying a pump action shotgun. "One of the men found this inside," he said.

Tanja gasped. "Is that it? Was he the one who shot at us?"

"Can't be sure yet," Diekmann said. "Don't worry, we'll find out. In the meantime, I've issued a B.O.L.O. We're going to look for some family, see if anyone has heard from him. I'm afraid there's not much more we can do at this point. The two of you might as well call it a day."

"Will you let us know as soon as you hear something?" Tanja said.

"Absolutely."

168

Half an hour later, we were back at home, staring at our empty fridge. "Do you think Diekmann will still pay us if they don't catch Mr. King?" Tanja said.

"Of course he will. He said we'd get paid to solve the case. We did that, didn't we?"

"I guess so. I hope you're right, Joe. We may be caught up on the mortgage now, but in thirty days, it will start all over again."

I put my arms around her and pulled her close. "I told you, everything is going to be fine. I told you we'd solve the case. We did. Now I'm telling you that Diekmann will pay us. We can trust him."

"I know," she said, dissolving into my chest. "Sometimes it's just too much."

"We still have some cash left in the bank," I said. "We can get some food."

"The Suburban is almost out of gas."

"Credit card."

"We're down to our last hundred dollars on the card."

"I said everything would be okay. I didn't say we weren't cutting it close."

"Joe, I want to go to bed."

"Are you serious? What about dinner?"

She pulled away and gave me a wincing look. "Can't I do both?"

I laughed. "This is way too much stress for you right now. Go get in bed. I'll run to the store."

"Are you sure? I can go with you."

"Don't make me pull rank," I said. "Get in bed. That's an order."

She cocked an eyebrow. "An order, huh? What if I make a run for it, tough guy? You gonna chase me down with your walker?"

"Shouldn't be hard, the way you waddle."

She punched me in the shoulder, giggling as she did it. I gave her one last kiss before walking out the door. On the way out, I set the alarm, just to be sure. I didn't think King would show back up at our house, but I wasn't taking any risks. I had a feeling that Tanja would be keeping her Glock close at hand as well.

Traffic was slow, and standing in line at the check-out was even slower. Five lanes were open, not counting the self-checks, and each had a line five customers deep. The self-checks were mostly empty, but that was no use to anyone because alcoholic beverages couldn't be purchased through self-check. That meant everyone who had any alcohol, as in my case, a six-pack of pale ale, had to wait in line.

By the time I was finally out of the store, it was pouring rain and the wind had begun to blow. I tossed the bag of groceries in the back, jumped into the driver's seat, and turned up the heat. All the way home, all I could think about was a warm meal, a cold beer, and crawling into bed with my wife. But as I pulled into our driveway, Tanja came running out the front door with her belly swaying back and forth and her hood pulled up over her head

"What are you doing?" I said as she jumped into the car.

"Joe, we have to go!"

"Go where? What's the matter?"

"After you left, I got to thinking about Mr. King. I was trying to figure out where he had gone. At first, I thought he was heading to another state to hide out with relatives. But of course, he knew that would be the first thing we expected, and if he had to give up his entire life, it would make more sense to leave the country."

"I know. That's why Diekmann issued a B.O.L.O."

"I know that, Joe. That's the problem. That's not where he's going."

"What are you talking about?"

"Think about it. If you were in his shoes, what would you do? Leave your whole life behind and make a run for another country, hoping not to get caught at the airport? Hoping that later on, you wouldn't be extradited back here anyway? Of course not! Why would King go through all that when all he really needs to do is get rid of the one last witness!"

"You think he went after Pishard?"

"I'm sure of it, Joe. I tried calling the cell phone number on the business card Pishard gave us but he didn't answer. Then I tried the boat dealership, but nobody was answering there, either."

I considered that. "It does seem odd that nobody would answer at the dealership. How late are they open?"

"His card says seven p.m. I think we should check there first."

I sighed, thinking of the cold six-pack in the back seat. I backed out of the driveway and headed for the onramp. "Are you sure we shouldn't just let them kill each other?" I grumbled.

"That is one more possibility we haven't even considered yet," Tanja said absently.

"What might that be?"

"Maybe they've been working together all along."

I tried to wrap my head around that. "I suppose it's just as possible as anything else. If it's true, then Pishard warned King the minute Diekmann cut him loose."

"Which may be exactly why we can't find either one of them."

"I like the idea of them killing each other better. I guess that would be just too easy."

"And far too satisfactory," Tanja said with a grin.

We pulled into the dealership at six p.m. The gate was open, and the lights were on. It was still raining, and Shane came out with an umbrella to greet us as we were parking. I rolled down the window far enough to talk. He recognized me instantly, and gave me a wary look.

"You need something?" he said.

"Is your boss here?"

"He headed out to Bodega a couple hours ago."

"Bodega?" Tanja said. "What for?"

"That's where our warehouse is."

"What's the address?"

"I'm not supposed to give out that information."

"If you're trying to protect your boss, you don't have to worry. This is for his safety."

"I'm afraid I can't help you."

"This is a criminal investigation," Tanja said. "If you don't give us that address, I'll make sure you're charged with obstruction."

"You're not even cops," he said with a sneer. "I should call the police and have them arrest you for harassment, and trespassing."

I opened the door and stepped out of the car. Staring at him with the rain pouring down over my face, I said, "You're right, we're not cops. Which means I can get away with all kinds of stuff cops can't."

"If you touch me, I'll sue."

"You don't have any witnesses, and I'm not leaving here without that address. So how do you want me to get it?"

He glanced around, and realized I was speaking the truth. No one was out in that rain, and if there was anyone in the office, they couldn't see us. If anything went down between the two of us, it was his word against mine. I let him assume my wife would side with me, which wasn't necessarily the case, but I wasn't going to tell him that.

"Seventy-five hundred Pelican Way."

"Thanks."

Shane went trudging through the rain back towards the office, presumably to call the police. I climbed back into the car and put it in gear.

"I keep warning you about your temper," Tanja said as I drove out of the lot.

"Relax, I didn't touch him."

"No, you didn't have to because he saw what happened when you *touched* his boss."

"That was self-defense."

"Do you have an answer to everything?"

"Do you have a complaint about everything?"

"It's my prerogative."

"You have a lot of those," I said, turning on the stereo.

I took the most direct route to Bodega Bay, which is about as direct as the flight path of a bumblebee on cocaine. Traffic on Highway 12 was smooth until just outside Sebastopol. Halfway through town, I merged onto Bodega Highway, a narrow, winding two-lane road that meanders through the countryside for about fifteen miles before dead-ending into Highway 1 at the coast.

Needless to say, even when traffic picked up, it was still slow going. The rain slacked off just enough for the fog to close in. The roads were slicker than snot on a glass doorknob, as Grandpa used to say, and visibility was down to a few yards.

Twenty minutes later, we hit Highway 1. The fog lifted, but as we left the shelter of the coastal hills, a gale force wind came roaring in off the Pacific. Between the wind and the driving rain, I had a tough time just keeping the Suburban between the lines.

"No signal," Tanja said, staring at her phone. "I was going to look the address up on a map."

"If I remember right, that road is a couple miles north of town."

"Do you think we should have called Diekmann?"

"I don't see what good it would have done. We don't even know if anybody's out here. Let's check it out first. If we need to, we'll drive around until we get a cell signal."

"What if we don't get a signal?"

"We can use a landline at one of these restaurants."

We passed through Bodega Bay, a quaint little town full of kite shops, candy stores, and art galleries. The place seemed ominous and foreboding with the storm raging, and everything dark and shuttered.

A few minutes later, I pulled onto Pelican Way. Two ridges rose up along either side of the road, perfectly funneling the wind up into the narrow valley. It was like driving through a hurricane. Two hundred yards up the road, we came to an eight-foot chain link fence surrounding a creepy-looking old warehouse. A bolt of lightning flashed across the sky, momentarily illuminating the area. I shut off the headlights.

"I'm going to sneak up there and take a look," I said.

"I'm coming with you."

"No, you're not. Remember what the doctor said? You're supposed to be taking it easy. You shouldn't even be here, much less sneaking around in the dark and the rain." I reached for the door handle and she put a hand on my arm.

"Joe, I don't like this."

"Relax, I'm just taking a look."

"What if somebody sees you?"

"You have your Glock, right? If anything happens, you can cover me on the way out."

"What if you don't come out?"

Tanja's eyes were huge, and I almost hesitated. She's a southern California girl. She's not used to the stormy isolation of the north coast, and I could tell she didn't want to be alone out there at night.

"I'll be fine," I promised, pulling her close. I could smell the perfume on her neck and the warmth of her skin drawing me in. I gave her a quick peck on the lips and pulled away while I still could. I opened the door.

"If I'm not back in fifteen minutes, get out of here. Drive up the road until you find a phone signal and call Diekmann. If you have to, go use a landline back in town."

I grabbed my cane and stepped out into the rain. It was coming down in sheets, and even though it was only a hundred yards away, the building was little more than a silhouette in a foggy haze. I saw a glimmer of light in one of the upper windows, and that's when it occurred to me that I didn't have my gun. I'd left it on the nightstand that morning.

I reminded myself that I was just going to take a look. Besides, I'd been through worse without a gun. I didn't consider either of those two much of a threat. King was old and frail and completely unfamiliar with physical violence, and Pishard... well, he had already proven his physical prowess, or lack thereof.

I slipped through the gate and moved along the fence line towards the building, hoping the distance and the storm would help to obscure me from sight. The rain had already soaked me to the bone and the wind was blowing so hard I had to lean into it and squint my eyes against the spray. My leg was tight and throbbing, and I was leaning heavily on my cane. All things considered, I still moved fairly quickly. The thought of reaching the shelter of the warehouse provided some motivation in that regard.

I reached a spot adjacent to the back corner of the building, and hurried across the parking lot. I pressed my back up against the wall and took a moment to catch my breath. The slope of the hillside channeled the wind up the hill behind me, whipping the sagebrush and wild grain into a frenzy. The gusts made a moaning sound through the rafters, and sent spirals of fog twisting up the hillside like dust devils.

I crept to the nearest window and tried to peek inside. Unfortunately, the window had been painted over. There was another a few yards down, but it looked the same, and the one after that had been boarded over. Frustrated, I moved around the far corner, looking for a way to make a quiet entrance. As I went around the building, the hillside closed in behind the warehouse and I found the area blessedly dry, but still freezing cold.

Just around the corner, I found a door. I twisted the handle and found the deadbolt had been locked. I pulled out my wallet and removed my lock picking kit. I inserted the pick and tension wrench, and began working my way slowly back and forth, trying to force the pins into place without making a noise that would tip off the occupants of the building.

With the wind howling around me, and the moisture running off my shaved head and into my eyes, it took a lot longer than it should have. It didn't help that I was very out of practice. I hadn't had to pick a lock in three years.

At last, I heard the telltale click and felt the lock begin to twist under slight pressure. Very gently, I turned the tension wrench and felt the deadbolt slide back. I winced as it made a slight *clicking* sound.

I shoved the picks into my back pocket and pulled the door open a crack. I was taking a risk that the building might have some sort of security system, but since someone was inside, the alarm had mostly likely been disabled. I peeked through the narrow slit and saw a dimly lit room full of boats, kayaks, and piles of miscellaneous junk. Most of the stuff looked pretty old.

This, I presumed was the final resting ground for all those old trade-ins. I drew the door open a little wider, giving my self a broader field of vision, and saw no signs of life. I stepped inside and pulled the door shut behind me.

There was something creepy about that place. All of those old boats rotting away under a thick layer of dust and spider webs gave me a chill. Some of those boats went back to the fifties. I saw everything from canoes to thirty-foot sailboats. Some of them were even custom made.

I felt a sad compulsion to rescue all of those poor old boats, like poor little orphans lost in the wilderness. It didn't make sense to me that they would be allowed to just sit and rot like that. I thought I knew why, though. Pishard didn't want those old boats floating around the classifieds. He wanted them out of commission, so that when people needed a boat, they'd have to go to him and buy a new one. There's nothing illegal about it. It's just a symptom of life in a disposable society.

I stepped around the hull of an old wooden powerboat and bent down, keeping my head low as I crossed the room. In the distance, near the front of the warehouse, I saw light streaming down a wooden staircase from the second floor. I worked my way slowly in that direction, careful not to bump into anything or trip over the many objects lying on the floor. That was easier said than done. Moving through that warehouse in the dark, trying to keep a low profile while leaning on my cane was tricky. Every few feet, I came across an old outboard engine or life preserver just lying on the floor. The place was like an obstacle course of derelict boating accessories.

By the time I got close to the staircase, I had the feeling my time was just about up. I felt a twinge of guilt as I thought of Tanja sitting alone in the dark, worrying about me. That was almost enough to make me turn back. But not this close. Not when I had already come this far...

I paused at the base of the staircase, straining to hear anything over the rain pounding down on the metal roof. If King and Pishard were up there, they weren't making much noise.

I cautiously took the first step. I moved my weight slowly, good leg first, then gradually lifted my left foot onto the step, putting my weight on the cane. I worked my way halfway up the staircase like that, practically crawling one step at a time, counting them out in the back of my head like an obsessive compulsive climbing the steps at Giza.

Number eight was the one that got me. I put my weight on that step, and it groaned like the Titanic smashing into an iceberg. I fought the urge to pull back. With my weight balanced uncomfortably between my good leg and my cane, I'd probably just end up falling down the stairs backwards.

I steadied myself and stood there, listening to the downpour, straining to hear anything that hinted I'd given myself away. A good minute passed that way. At last, I took another step. Number eight creaked slightly as I shifted my weight, but not nearly as loudly as the first time.

At last, I reached the height of the upper floor. I leaned up against the wall, and ever so carefully took a peak over the top. I saw a large, mostly empty room. Papers covered the walls, possibly blueprints for various boats. There was a desk against the far wall. Opposite the desk, just a few yards away from me, was a chair. It was facing away from me, but I was sure the man sitting in it was James Pishard. Or, it *had been* Pishard, judging by the pool of blood on the floor around him.

"There you are, Mr. Shepherd," said a familiar voice behind me. I nearly jumped out of my skin. I turned to see Mr. King at the far end of the stairwell, overlooking the staircase. He must have been hiding back there the whole time, waiting for me to get to the top of the stairwell.

"Come on up," he said. "Where is that pretty wife of yours?"

"She didn't come."

"Perfect! This will be so much simpler that way."

I climbed to the top of the stairs and lurched over to the chair. Pishard's head lolled uncomfortably off to the side, his death gaze fixed on some distant point beyond the ceiling. The blood was already darkening around the bullet wound in his temple.

"Nine millimeter," Mr. King said. "Very fast, very clean. James chose an excellent weapon for his suicide, don't you think?"

"Is that the same gun you used on the reporter?"

"Aren't you the clever one?"

"If you think killing Pishard is going to get you off, you haven't thought this through very well. He's not the only one who knows what you did."

"First of all, I didn't kill Pishard. He killed himself, right after he killed you. He couldn't take the guilt anymore, which is exactly what I plan to write in his suicide note. And yes, I have thought this through. See, Pishard was the only witness left. I was sure he'd keep his mouth shut after what happened to Richard, but I guess he got brave. It was bound to happen eventually. See, children can be controlled. They don't understand the world. They don't know who they can trust, or what might happen to them if they're not careful. All it takes is a few words, a few seeds whispered into their fertile young minds...

"But they inevitably grow up. That's the tragedy of it all. They lose their fear, their malleability. Slowly, over the years, they turn into the thing that they hate most. They turn into *their parents*. They start feeling responsible, and they're staring down the barrel of middle age, and suddenly they have a crisis of conscience. They start thinking maybe they should go to the cops about that thing that happened so long ago.

"It doesn't matter, though. There is more than one way to skin a cat, Mr. Shepherd. After tonight, I can finally put this story to rest once and for all."

"That's not gonna happen," I said. "Pishard confessed. The sheriff knows everything."

"Really?" he said with a devious smile. "After the sheriff sees what Pishard has done tonight, do you think that confession will mean anything?"

He had a point. The whole murder/suicide scheme was simple but effective. I almost wished he had come up with something more elaborate. That way, there would have been at least some margin for error.

I took a deep breath and told myself that Tanja was just a few miles away, calling Diekmann that very minute. She must have realized by then that something had happened; that she needed to go for help. It didn't make much difference, though. It would be at least twenty minutes before Diekmann showed up. By then, I'd be dead and King would be long gone. At least Tanja would be safe.

"Take a few steps to your left, if you please," King said. "That spot looks about right, don't you think?"

"First tell me what happened," I said. "What made you kill Myles Meyer? Did he threaten to blackmail you?"

"No, it was nothing like that. Myles was a good boy, pure, unsullied. It was something rare and wonderful then, almost nonexistent now. The two of us, we had an understanding. I could tell by the way he looked

181

at me, by the way that he talked to me... he *understood*."

"What? That you're a pedophile?"

"Don't. Just don't. At his age, he was almost a man. He was no innocent. He'd been trying to get my attention for weeks. He was jealous of the other boys."

"Why kill him?" I said. "You don't expect me to believe it was just an accident."

"But it was. Can't you understand that? That's the tragedy of this whole thing!"

"How do you accidentally kill someone?"

"Myles and I had been waiting so long for the chance to be alone. When it finally happened, it was like destiny. It was karma. But Myles was nervous; afraid we might be caught, and he started to struggle. I didn't know what to do. This boy who had been leading me on for weeks was about to ruin everything. When people found out, it would have been the end of my career. It would have ruined me.

"I panicked. I tried to put my hand over his mouth, just to keep him quiet until I could calm him down. In our struggle, he threw his head back and somehow struck a sharp rock. It killed him. It was a freak accident, something that would have just bruised ninety-nine percent of us. But for Myles... it must have been his time. I can't imagine how else it could have happened. Just a horrible, horrible accident. That's how it all began."

"Pishard was telling the truth," I said. "And after Myles died, you convinced the other boys to help you hide the body?"

"Yes. We all knew it was for the best. We swore each other to secrecy. We would never speak of it again."

"But Richard broke that oath?"

"He was going to. He called me one day, out of the blue. Said he couldn't take the guilt anymore. He had become a man, raised a child of his own. He said it wasn't right, leaving that body up there on the hill. He said that we had to do the right thing. Of course, I knew what that really meant. It meant he was going to tell the truth, and when the police investigated, they would find out everything. They would know I had been there; what I had been doing..."

"So you killed Richard before he could talk. You made it look like a suicide."

"Yes, and that should have been the end of it. It really should have. I don't know why his daughter wouldn't get that silly notion about his murder out of her head. Becky went through counseling. We all told her that she needed to accept his death and move on. She just wouldn't."

"How did you know about her and Randall?"

"Oh, I knew Becky was up to something the first day Randall came to the high school. I had seen the two of them talking. After he left, she said something into her voice recorder. I had this terrible feeling it was about her father, and I was right.

"I started to keep an eye on her. The night she met Randall, I was there. He had brought some digging equipment, which they put in her car, and they drove up to the reservoir together. As soon as they parked, I knew what I had to do. I had my pistol with me, so I shot Randall."

"And Becky tried to run away?"

"Yes. I chased her down the hill, into the dairy. She tried to hide inside the building, but I found her."

183

"And you attacked her, and dumped her into the vat?"

"Yes. I had planned to bring her body up to the car, but before I could, that half-wit came around. He was calling all the cows in to the milking machines."

"So you panicked and threw Becky into the cream?"

"What else could I do? I dumped her into the vat, closed the lid, and snuck back up to the hill. I had to cover my tracks before anyone saw me there. I put the reporter's body in the car. I drove it over to the dock, and let it roll right into the lake."

"The voice recorder..." I mumbled.

"What?"

"Becky confronted you, and you threatened to kill her. She recorded the whole conversation."

"You're mistaken," he said.

I considered that. "It must have been Pishard then... he was warning her away, wasn't he?"

"Sounds like the sort of thing he would do. I should have killed that fool years ago."

I smiled. I had started talking with the hope of buying myself some time. I hadn't expected King to give me a full confession. I just had to keep him talking a bit longer... ten minutes, maybe. Fifteen?

Then I heard the loud, unmistakable creaking sound of step number eight.

Chapter 13

Tanja

I wish I could say I was surprised that Joe didn't come back when he said he would, but I wasn't. That's just the kind of thing Joe does. You know the type. He leaps headfirst into dangerous situations without a second thought for his own well-being, and hardly a thought for anyone else. He thrives on dangerous situations. He's an Alpha.

It's not entirely Joe's fault. He spent so many years working undercover that all he knows now is how to follow his instincts. He's not used to working with a partner, much less being married to one, and he sure doesn't think things through before he acts. I suppose I can forgive him, since that's probably what has kept him alive this long. He is getting better about it. But at times -like when he jumped out of the car and went rushing off into the storm- I just want to strangle him.

"Give me fifteen minutes," he had said. *Sure Joe, great plan.* Except that even if I could get a cell signal in that storm, it would have taken Diekmann twenty-five minutes to get there. And where would that leave us, you reckless imbecile? Ah, well. I suppose that's the price we pay for marriage. We put up with men being imbeciles and they put up with us and our hormones. When you add it all up, I'm still fairly certain that women drew the short straw on that deal. At least we only act like idiots once a month.

So I did what came naturally: the exact opposite of what he told me to do! Glock in hand, I followed Joe's path around the outside edge of the property. I crept along the fence line to the back of the warehouse, right up to the back door on the far side. It was still unlocked, having been left that way by my careless, erratic, semi-crippled husband. I slipped quietly inside.

The place had given me chills just looking at it from the outside. Inside, it was like walking through a crypt. It was a graveyard of ghost ships, dozens of vessels of every type and size, abandoned and forgotten, left to rot away to nothing inside some dark old warehouse. I kept expecting to look into one of the boats and see a skeleton with a captain's hat grinning back at me. Part of me wanted to run shrieking out of there. Another part wanted to find a match and burn the place to the ground.

Halfway across the room, I paused to pull a cobweb from my hair and I heard voices drifting down from above. The web tugged at my hair as I pulled on it, and clung to the skin of my shoulders. I ignored the creeping sensation that crawled up my spine and pushed forward, straining to hear the conversation over the racket of the building's metal roof in the storm. I recognized Joe's voice, but the other was muffled. I couldn't tell if it was King or Pishard. It had to be one of those two.

I made my way to the staircase, dodging around rotten old life vests and the carcass of a wooden kayak, and began climbing the stairs.

"Nine millimeter," King's voice said. "James chose an excellent weapon for his suicide, don't you think?"

Suicide? My breath caught in my chest. We were too late. King had already killed Pishard. Now he was going to kill Joe. I raised my Glock to eye level as the top of the stairwell came into view. I saw Joe's legs, and a chair next to him. I took another step.

Creak! The sound of the stair groaning under my weight sent my stomach churning. I heard a noise behind me and swung around to see Solomon King lurking at the edge of the stairwell behind a partial wall. He was carrying a pistol.

King fired a shot, but not at me. He was aiming at Joe. The explosion of gunfire shocked my eardrums and filled my ears with a loud, pulsating tone. I spun around, leveling my sights on the teacher, and squeeze-ed the trigger. Plaster exploded and King dropped out of sight. I ran to the top of the stairs and saw Joe's face peering out from behind Pishard's body.

"Move!" he shouted at the top of his lungs. His gaze flashed over my shoulder, and I knew King was taking aim at me. I dropped to one knee and rolled sideways.

As I landed, I felt something tear inside me. I cried out and dropped the pistol, clutching at my belly. A warm gush of fluid went rushing down my thighs. A contraction came out of nowhere, forcing an involuntary scream out of my lungs.

I heard another gunshot, like a distant *pop!* Be-neath the ringing in my ears. In the corner of my eyes, I saw Joe drop. I turned, half-expecting to see my husband lying on the floor dead from a bullet wound. Instead, he was crawling towards me.

King fired another shot. The bullet came so close that I felt the wind of it against my hair. The floor-boards exploded between us, and we both flinched as slivers of wood sprayed up into the air. Joe lunged for my gun. He rolled onto his side, leveled the sights, and

187

began squeezing the trigger. The teacher leapt back out of sight, but I knew Joe had hit him at least once because I heard a scream. The sound was cut short, and I heard and felt the *thud* of King's body hitting the floor. Joe looked back at me. His eyes widened as he realized my predicament.

"Are you okay?" I could barely hear his words over the ringing in my ears, but I understood. I nodded.

"I think so," I said, wincing as another small contraction rolled over me.

Joe pulled my head onto his lap. From that angle, I could see King's motionless legs sticking out from behind the wall. I looked up into Joe's face and saw him staring down at me.

"What happened?" he said, brushing my hair out of my eyes. "Are you all right?"

"My water broke," I said. "Joe, I think the baby is coming!"

His eyes lit up in a panic. "Hang on," he said, trying to twist out from underneath me. "I'm going to get you out of here!"

"No, there's no time for that. We have to do it here."

"What? We can't just... where's your phone? I'll call an ambulance!"

"There's no signal," I said. I breathed in deeply as the contractions subsided. "Relax, Joe. We can handle this. First, find me something to lie back on."

"Like what?"

"Anyth-" I started to say, but another contraction cut me off. It was a behemoth. Spasms racked my entire body. I reached up, grabbing him by the collar, gasping for breath. Just as it began to fade, another hit me like a semi-truck. The pain rolled over my body. It gradually subsided, and I realized I had been screaming. I wasn't sure exactly when I had started.

"What the...!" Joe shouted. "Are you okay?"

"Contractions," I said when I could breathe again. "Remember, Joe? Remember the classes we took?"

"Okay, let me think..." He took me by the hand. "Here, squeeze my hand. Now, breathe!"

"I am breathing, you idiot! Get me a pillow before I squeeze something else that you won't like!"

Joe went scurrying across the room. He came back a few seconds later with a padded desk chair. He turned it upside down on the floor, and helped me lean back against it. It doesn't sound very comfortable, but it was an adjustable reclining chair. Joe managed to get enough of an angle that I could relax a little. After getting me settled, he took my hand again, and wiped my bangs from my eyes.

"Okay, deep breaths. You're doing great. You're going to be fine."

I started screaming my way through another contraction as a security guard appeared at the top of stairs. He was young, overweight, and dressed in a blue uniform clearly at least one size too small. He glanced at Pishard's body and swung his flashlight in our direction, nearly blinding me with the light of a thousand suns.

"TURN THAT OFF!" I screamed. The guy just stared at us, blinking. Joe told him to shut it off, or he would do something both profane and anatomically impossible. The guard finally got the hint. I was only vaguely aware of the conversation that followed:

"Sorry," the guard mumbled, flicking the switch. He licked his lips and threw his gaze around the room. "What in the world happened here?"

"She's in labor!" Joe barked. "Get us some help!"

"Should I radio for an ambulance?"

"Yes! No, wait. The Bodega Fire department. Call them. They're closest. And call Sheriff Diekmann."

"What about... that guy?" the guard said, glancing at Pishard's body.

"I'll make sure he doesn't go anywhere," Joe said.

The guard seemed to accept that answer. He went running down the stairs. Somehow, I managed a hoarse laugh.

"This isn't nearly how I imagined this," I said, my voice little more than a whisper.

"Nothing ever is," Joe said. "Don't worry, you're doing great."

"Joe, I'm sorry."

"What are you talking about?"

"Grandma. The mortgage. I should have told you."

"There's nothing to be sorry for. You panicked, that's all. It happens." I started to cry.

"I'm no good at this, Joe. I don't know how to be a wife, or a mom."

Joe laughed, but his eyes were glistening with moisture. "Stop it. You're the perfect wife. You are going to make a great mom."

"You think?"

"Absolutely."

"How do you know? After all the mistakes I've made..."

"What mistakes? Listen, the fact that you *want* to be a good mom tells me that you will be."

"I hope so. I don't want to let Autumn down."

"We won't. We'll give her everything a kid could want."

I groaned as another contraction came, but it was a small one and quickly receded. I took a few deep breaths. Joe had my right hand in his. With his left, he reached over to wipe the tears from my cheeks.

"This changes everything," I said in a whisper. "Everything, forever."

"For the better," he said.

Another contraction came and I lost track of our conversation.

"I see her!" Joe shouted somewhere in the hazy distance. "I can see the baby's head. Push, Tanja. Push now!"

I gasped as the next contraction came. I screamed, and pushed so hard I thought my guts were falling out. I felt my body ripping apart. Violent searing fire burned through my nerves. My hands clawed at the floor, and everything else in the world disappeared. Everything except for the pain. Everything melted together.

Hold, breathe, push... Scream!
Count. Breathe. Push. SCREAM!

Nine days later, baby Autumn was born.

Well, it felt like nine days. In reality, the entire thing was over in less than an hour. In that time -in that split universal second- everything I ever knew or thought I knew about life had changed. The storm went calm, and for a few minutes, the light of the full moon broke through the clouds. The whole universe seemed to take a breath.

Autumn screamed at first, and then fell silent as I put her to my breast. Joe put his arms around us, and kept us warm. As our precious newborn baby drifted off to sleep, I once again became aware of my surroundings. A few yards away, I saw Pishard's body resting in the chair where he had been murdered. At some point, Joe had pushed the chair back to the far wall, and turned it away from us so it wouldn't disturb me.

I looked over at the stairwell, and saw the craters in the sheetrock from the bullets Joe and I had fired at Mr. King. I glanced at the floor, where King's legs had been clearly visible after Joe shot him.

"Joe?"

"What is it, sweetness?"

"Where is King?"

Joe followed my stare. He leapt to his feet with my gun in hand and raced over to the stairwell, limping on his sore leg. He peered cautiously around the corner, and turned back to stare at me.

"He's gone!"

Chapter 14

Joe

Tanja's Glock had two bullets left in the magazine. I pulled back the slide, chambering a round so that it would be ready to fire. I knelt down, and put it in Tanja's free hand.

"Joe, what are you doing?"

I leaned close, pulling my jacket up over her and the baby. "I have to make sure King's gone," I said. "He may still be in here. We don't dare leave until we know for sure."

Her eyes widened slightly. Tanja's smooth skin was pale and her eyes glistened in the dim light. She was beautiful; more beautiful than I could ever remember. I was more in love with her at that moment than I had ever been in my life. I kissed her on the lips, and bent down to kiss Autumn on the forehead. My baby girl flinched at the touch of my whiskers, and began to burrow into Tanja's breast.

"Be careful," Tanja said. She placed the gun on the floor next to her so she could graze her fingers along my cheek.

"Don't worry, I won't let him hurt you. Either of you."

I pushed to my feet, and felt a sharp pain in my hip as I rose. I winced, glancing at my cane lying on the floor next to Tanja. I didn't pick it up. I wanted both hands free.

I limped over to the stairs and peered down into the darkened storage area. The patter of a light rain on the tin roof filled my ears. I saw a drop of blood a few steps down. The shadows swallowed up the stairs. I grabbed the handrail and slowly began my descent into that eerie nautical graveyard, one awkward step at a time.

Without my cane, the handrail had to bear a good portion of my weight. Thankfully, it was stable enough to withstand the pressure. I paused halfway down, turning my head side to side, scanning the dark, ghostly hulls for any sign of the killer. Through the windows at the front of the warehouse, I caught a glimpse of the cars sitting out front. That confirmed my suspicion. Solomon King was still in there with us somewhere, and he had a gun.

I thought back to our encounter, trying to remember how many shots he had fired. At least four, maybe five. I couldn't be sure. I thought the pistol he was carrying might be a Berretta. It was a nine millimeter, and depending on the model and year, the thing might hold as many as sixteen rounds. There was no doubt about it, I was in trouble.

I continued my descent, carefully skipping over number eight as I came to it, and then moved as quickly as I could to bottom of the stairs. A powerboat rose up to my left. I knelt down next to it, wincing as my hip cried out in pain.

I was just beyond the column of light shining down from the second floor, making it impossible for my eyes to adjust to the darkness. I moved slowly around the bow of the boat, deeper into the darkness of the warehouse.

I hid myself in the pitch-black shadow of two large sailboats, and waited quietly for my eyes to adjust. My other senses came to life. I became very aware of the scents of dust and grease and oiled wood. I heard a quiet *crack* across the room, or possibly outside. I couldn't tell which. The sound of the rain grew louder.

I moved along the length of the sailboats in that direction. As I came around the stern on my right, I saw the still form of a body lying on the floor in a dark pool of blood. Even in the darkness, I instantly recognized the security guard. I hurried to his side, lowering myself as far as I could manage without my hip giving out on me.

I grimaced as I saw the torn flesh on the guard's throat, and noticed the boathook lying on the concrete floor next to him. I felt a horrifying chill crawl down my spine as I realized the full depth of King's depravity. I had known the man was capable of murder, but the sheer violence of the act made my guts churn. King had ripped out the man's jugular just to avoid firing a shot and alerting us to his presence.

I searched the body, hoping to find a gun or a tazer, but came up empty. I picked up the flashlight that had fallen on the concrete floor next to him. I hesitated a moment, and then picked up the boathook, too.

"King!" I shouted into the air, turning my head so as to throw my voice around the room. "I know you're in here!"

I crept back into the shadow between the two sailboats and waited, listening intently, every muscle taught. I held the boathook in my right hand and the flashlight in my left. I had decided that I might be able to blind King with the flashlight long enough to use the hook on him. What might happen after that, remained to be seen.

At that moment, I was acutely aware of the fact that I might have to take a bullet for Tanja and Autumn. I was okay with that. The only thing I cared about was making sure that King couldn't hurt them. I was more than willing to die in order to ensure their safety. If I had to, I might even do what he had done to the guard. I didn't like the idea, but such moral principles fade into irrelevance when it comes to protecting your family.

I heard a sound up above me, and swung around just in time to see King's dark shape looming over me. He had climbed up into one of the sailboats. I saw his hand go up, and I leapt to the side as he fired a shot. The muzzle flare lit up the room. I landed awkwardly on my side and grunted as jolts of pain shot up and down my leg. I turned the flashlight on, and pointed it at him. The beam illuminated the deck of the boat, but King was gone.

I turned the light back off and crawled backwards, around the second boat, looking for cover. I couldn't see a thing. I clutched the boathook as if it was the fine line between life and death. Maybe it was.

"Joe!" King's voice said somewhere very close. "Joe, I can see you!"

I pushed painfully to my feet, wincing. I turned slowly, my ears straining to locate him. *Say something else!* I thought. *Just one more word.*

I heard a noise behind me, and spun around to see the dark silhouette of King's figure outlined against the hull of another boat. I struck out with the boathook just as he fired, and in the momentary flash of light, I saw the crazed look in his eyes. The shot missed, but I did too. I struck at him again, aiming for the space where I'd seen the muzzle flash. I was rewarded by the violent *thwack* of metal against bone.

King cried out, and I heard the gun clatter to the floor. I hit the switch on the flashlight, trying to blind him. King leapt on me, and we went down in a heap. My leg twisted as I fell, and an involuntary cry of pain escaped my lips. King took heart in this, laughing wickedly as he climbed up to straddle my chest, and started punching me in the face.

I had to release my grip on the boathook. It was too long to use in close quarters combat. King hit me with another fierce blow to the nose, and stars filled my vision. I struck out blindly with the flashlight, and hit him on the shoulder. I swung again, but King caught my arm in both hands.

Having released my grip on the boathook, I was free to swing at him with my right hand. I delivered a glancing right hook that had little effect, and King threw his head back, guarding his face with his arms. The flashlight was impeding my ability to fight, so I let it go. I thought this would allow me to strike him in the face.

King thwarted my plan. He took control of the flashlight. Using it as a weapon, he brought it down on my thigh as hard as he could. I roared, blinded by pain. I reached out, trying to latch onto him. As my hand closed on his shirt, King raised the flashlight over my head.

Seeing what he intended to do, I struggled frantic- ally, trying to find enough movement to avoid the inevitable skull-crushing blow. I pushed back at him, and King swung the flashlight violently down towards my face. At the same moment, there was a flash of light accompanied by the explosive report of gunfire.

King lurched. His swing went wide, and the flashlight tumbled out of his feeble grasp. The teacher went completely still, and I felt warm liquid dripping down from his chest onto my face. He fell sideways, dropping to the floor.

Behind him, I saw my wife's silhouette, one hand brandishing her Glock, the other clutching our little baby to her chest. I moaned painfully as I crawled out from underneath King's legs. I grabbed the flashlight, and put two fingers on his throat, checking for a pulse. There wasn't one. King had an exit wound the size of a golf ball in the center of his chest. I looked up at Tanja.

"You shouldn't be walking."

"I'm fine," she said.

I noticed the low ringing in my eardrums from the gunshot. "The baby... her ears." I pushed to my feet, grunting, trying to ignore the throbbing pain in my hip.

"It's okay," Tanja said, pulling back the jacket so I could see Autumn's face. "She's still asleep."

I leaned closer, frowning. "How in the...?" Then I saw the bright orange earplugs jammed into Autumn's tiny, perfect little ears. A look of confused amazement washed over my features. "I forgot you had those."

"It wasn't easy getting them in," she explained. "Autumn's ears are tiny. I guess it worked, though."

I turned the flashlight, throwing the beam across King's lifeless body.

"That was a good shot," I said. "Clever, coming down here after me. Did you have that planned the whole time?"

Tanja grinned wickedly. "Sorry for using you as bait. Somebody in this relationship has to do the thinking."

For the second time that week, Tanja and I spent the night in the hospital. Only this time, we weren't a couple. We were a *family*. It's impossible to describe the way my life changed that night. I had nine months to prepare for that day, yet I still felt like it came out of nowhere. Suddenly, relatives were calling and showing up at the hospital, bringing gifts and flowers, taking pictures. It was a whirlwind that I wasn't really prepared for. After all that had happened in the last few days, I couldn't do much but sit there and just watch everything happening around me.

Sometime around noon the next day, the nurse chased everybody out so we could have some quiet time before going home. She brought us lunch trays, but I had no interest. I laid back in the chair with Autumn sleeping on my chest while Tanja pecked at our food. Diekmann stuck his head through the door with a grin a mile wide, and Tanja waved him in.

"How is she doing?" he said in a whisper.

"Great!" Tanja said. "Look at her, she's a daddy's girl."

"Of course she is," I said, chuckling. "She knows who the man of the house is."

"Sure she does," said Diekmann. "And pretty soon she'll be telling the man of the house exactly what to do."

"What's going to happen now?" Tanja said. "I mean with the case?"

Diekmann grinned as he settled into one of the guest chairs. "I suppose it's closed. I hired you to find out who killed Becky Sweet. You did that, and then some."

"Not exactly," I said. "We know it had to be either King or Pishard, but we can't prove which one."

"It had to be King," Tanja said. "He knew about Becky's investigation into her father's murder. He's the one who would have known the reporter was helping her."

"Ah, but that's not all," Diekmann said with a sly grin. "On a hunch I ran the serial number on that old revolver, the one Becky's father supposedly used to kill himself."

"Was it registered?" I said.

"Nope, but the D.O.J. keeps a record of every gun sale in the state. Guess who I traced it back to."

"Mr. King?" said Tanja.

Diekmann shook his head. "James Pishard."

"Then Pishard killed Becky's father," Tanja said, her eyes growing wide. "Then that means the two of them had to be working together!"

"I'm sure of it," said Diekmann.

"It does make sense," I said. "If you think about it, Pishard was sleazy enough to try and pin Becky's murder on his own son. He must have done that because he knew the investigation would go nowhere."

"But all along he was lying to protect himself," said Diekmann. "And that's why the two of them killed Richard. That part of Pishard's story was true. Richard was going to rat them out, so they killed him. Then Becky came along, and started getting too close to the truth."

"And it all started with an accident," Tanja said. "One accident led to all those murders."

"It's not over yet," said Diekmann. "My office has been getting discomforting phone calls all morning."

"Phone calls?" I said. "About what?"

"Your story made it into the papers. Several parents saw it, and called to tell us they believe Mr. King may have been sexually abusing their kids. As the word gets out, I expect we may be hearing more of that."

"How horrible," said Tanja.

"Oh, and one more thing..." he reached into his shirt pocket and produced a check that he handed to Tanja. "This is your fee."

Tanja accepted it, and gasped as she read it. "Sheriff, this is for eight thousand dollars!"

"The way I see it, you didn't just solve the one case I asked you to... you solved four murders. I'm paying you for all four cases. That's the good news. The bad news is that I'm officially tapped out. I won't have any more money in the coffers until the new fiscal year, so you two better make good of all this publicity."

"Publicity?" said Tanja.

"Do you remember Mary Sinclair, the reporter? She'll be following up on that TV interview, and she won't be the only one. I expect your phone will be ringing off the hook by the time you get home. Think you'll be up for it?"

"I think we'll get some sleep first," I said, glancing down at my baby girl.

Tanja sighed and leaned back against her pillow.

"Joe?"

"Yes, dear?"

"Take me home. I want to hold my baby and stare out the window at the redwoods."

Chapter 15

Tanja

All's well that ends well. Isn't that how the old saying goes? Of course, if you've learned anything about Joe, you already know that wasn't quite the end. Not yet. The real end came three weeks later.

We were at home. I had just put Autumn down for a nap in her room and Joe was in the living room, messing around on the computer. I poured a cup of coffee and went to see what he was working on. I found him surfing the *Sequoia Marine Sports* website.

"I thought they went out of business," I said.

"They did. When Pishard died, that was the end of the company. The insurance company is auctioning off all the inventory."

"Don't get any ideas," I said.

The rumble of a diesel engine out front and the squealing sound of brakes interrupted our conversation. Joe's eyes lit up, and he jumped out of the chair.

"It's here!" he said, running for the door.

"What? What's here?"

I stared after him as he yanked the front door open and went racing outside. Tentatively, I pulled the living room curtains aside. I saw Diekmann's old yellow truck out there. Behind it, on a rusty old trailer, rested a blue and white sailboat. I closed my eyes and took a deep breath. When I opened them back up, I saw Joe waving at me from the lawn.

"Check it out!" he shouted. "Tanja, get out here!"

I looked at the computer again and realized that Joe had been shopping for life vests and boat accessories. I heard baby Autumn cooing in the back room, and I hurried to pick her up. When I reached the crib, she was smiling up at me, her beautiful blue eyes sparkling in the afternoon light.

"Couldn't sleep?" I said, picking her up. "I'm not surprised. I have a feeling your daddy isn't going to let me get any sleep for a long time, either."

The phone rang in the next room, and I hurried to pick it up.

"Hello?" I said.

"May I speak to Joe Shepherd?" said a woman's voice. I frowned.

"He can't come to the phone. Can I take a message?"

"Yes, please tell him Madelyn Cook called to confirm his therapy appointment for tomorrow afternoon."

"He'll be there," I said with a smile turning up the corners of my mouth. "Count on it."

The End

Keep reading for a look into the origin of Joe and Tanja's relationship...

Bonus Material:

The Interview

By Mary Sinclair for Channel 7 News, Santa Rosa

Mary: Today, I'm interviewing Joe and Tanja Shepherd, the owners of Sequoia County's newest small business, the *Autumn's Hope Detective Agency*. Let's start at the beginning: How did the two of you get into the business of private investigation? It seems an unlikely choice for a young couple.

Joe: It's a long story. We were both in law enforcement, and that's how we met.

Mary: Did you work together?

Tanja: No, I was a Behavior Analyst for the FBI

Joe: She really gets into a person's head. My wife can have a thirty-second conversation with a suspect and know everything about him.

Mary: Is that true?

Tanja: Joe is exaggerating. I simply observe a person's body language, clothing, and so forth. I use that information to read a suspect. It's a skill I've developed over many years.

Mary: Don't be offended if I sound skeptical, but is it really possible to learn so much just from watching a person?

Tanja: You'd be surprised.

Mary: Alright... how about a demonstration?

Tanja glances at Joe. After an encouraging nod from her spouse, she begins to speak:

Tanja: You're between the ages of twenty-eight and thirty. You're single, have no kids, and you've never been married. You try to eat a healthy diet, but you starve yourself to stay fit, and you drink too much alcohol. You also like to tan, but you haven't had time to lately. You drive a BMW, and you graduated from UC Berkeley.

Mary: Oh. My. God.

Joe: *(laughing)* She's just getting warmed up.

Tanja: Should I go on?

Mary: *(somewhat embarrassed)* No, thank you very much. Did you really just imagine all of that?

Tanja: No, not imagined. Extrapolated.

Mary: From what?

Tanja: When Joe and I arrived for this interview, there were only three cars in the lot. It was logical to assume one of them belonged to you. The nicest was a BMW, which incidentally has a UC Berkeley sticker on the bumper. That vehicle seemed most likely owned by the highest ranking -and therefore highest paid-employee here today. Since you are the reporter and the others here are supporting staff, I naturally presumed the Beemer was yours. Later, as we passed your desk, I saw the BMW keychain hanging out of your purse and confirmed my suspicions.

I also saw that you had pictures of your parents in your office, but no photographs of children or a spouse. Also, you're not wearing a wedding ring, and haven't had a ring on that finger in some time, if ever. However, Valentine's Day is this weekend and the fresh bouquet of roses and the box of chocolates on your desk implies that you have some sort of suitor. Probably male, based on the type of gift, and based on the way you looked at my husband when you thought I wasn't looking.

Mary: Excuse me?

Tanja: It's a perfectly normal reaction for a single woman. Married women do this also, without even realizing what they're doing.

Mary: They do what, exactly?

Tanja: This is where the body language ties it all together. When we first met, you glanced at Joe, then at me, then at him again. You did a double take. The second time, you held your gaze. This action was subtle and probably subconscious, but it told me that you find Joe attractive and that you were *sizing him up*, so to speak. You also focused mostly on Joe during our conversation. You turned slightly to the side, opening yourself to him, while presenting your shoulder to me, a sign that you were subconsciously brushing me aside, or at least making Joe the focus of your attention.

Mary: I'm sorry if I did that. I didn't mean to offend you.

Tanja: *(waving Mary's concerns aside)* Not at all. Like I said, most of these actions are subconscious. The fact that you give out subconscious signals doesn't necessarily imply you are willing to act on them. It simply means that you're human; that you experience and react to emotions, just as we all do.

Mary: That's a relief.

Tanja: Body language is really only half of it. The other half is observation. When you combine these skills, you can extrapolate information that no one would ever suspect.

Mary: Amazing. What about you, Joe? What kind of work do you do?

Joe: I was on the state's Organized Crime Task Force. I've worked independently and in cooperation with other state and federal agencies, like the CBI, the ATF, the FBI, ICE, and a few others.

Mary: That's a lot of letters. What exactly did you do?

Joe: *(hesitates a moment before answering)* I worked undercover.

Mary: So you're like one of those guys in the movies? The ones who change their appearance and try to blend in with a gang, in order to catch the bad guys?

Joe: Something like that. It was my job to infiltrate different groups for various reasons. Sometimes we were running an investigation, looking for a specific person, other times we were just running a sweep, casting a wide net over as many criminals as possible.

Mary: That sounds very dangerous.

Joe: I've had close calls.

Mary: Is that what happened to your leg? I noticed when you came in for the interview that you were using a cane.

Joe: That happened on my very last case with the task force; the one where I met Tanja.

Mary: What happened?

(Joe glances at Tanja, and she takes up the story)

Tanja: Well, first of all, Joe and I did *not* get along at first. In fact, the first time we met, I arrested him. *(They both laugh.)*

Mary: Really?

Joe: She didn't go easy on me, either. She called me a "scumbag" and nearly broke my arm cuffing me.

Tanja: He makes it sound so dramatic. Truth is, he was working undercover, so I had no idea who he really was. We just happened to be investigating the same gang. My team raided one of his gang's facilities, and Joe got caught up in the mix. I saw him making a run for it, so I blindsided him.

Mary: That's quite a story. It's hard to imagine how the two of you ended up being married.

Tanja: Well, you asked about Joe's leg. That was because of me. It happened when he was trying to save me. In fact, if Joe hadn't gone over that roof, I might not be here today.

Mary: So he saved your life?

Tanja: Absolutely. He tackled the guy who was going to shoot me, and they both went off the roof of a four-story building. They landed on a parked car, with Joe on top.

Joe: *(displaying his cane)* I got hurt, but I survived. The other guy wasn't so lucky.

Mary: I see.

Tanja: I went to see Joe in the hospital that night, and he asked me to marry him.

Mary: How romantic.

Joe: It wasn't *that* romantic. She said "No."

Mary: Seriously?

Joe: Seriously.

Tanja: Please, Joe. You were high on morphine. I was probably the third woman you had proposed to that night.

Mary: I don't understand. If you didn't get together that night, then when?

Tanja: After the incident, Joe's team leader and my Special Agent in Charge came to an agreement to cooperate on the case. We were looking for a very specific criminal, someone Joe already had access to. I thought it was a bad idea, but it wasn't my call. They more or less forced us to work together.

Mary: I see. So that was the source of the tension between the two of you?

Tanja: Yes, that and his cocky attitude, and his recklessness.

Joe makes an exaggerated snort.

Tanja: Joe's cover got blown. The gang decided to torture him for information. They were going to kill him, but my team figured out where Joe was being held, and we rescued him. That's all. I was just doing my job.

Joe: (*leans forward and whispers:*) She doesn't like to admit it, but she was madly in love with me from the first time we met.

Tanja: Oh, stop. Your ego is about to bust out the windows.

Joe: (*Joe looks at Tanja, his blue eyes twinkling, a mischievous grin playing across his face.*) Yeah? So how come *you* proposed to *me?*

(Tanja rolls her eyes)

Mary: So you both saved each other?

Tanja: Yes, you could say that.

Mary: So what about the detective agency? How did that get started?

Joe: After the accident, I couldn't work undercover anymore because my leg never healed right. The doctors knew it was going to give me trouble for the rest of my life. Some days I can walk okay, but when there's a storm coming, I might as well be in a wheelchair. The task force offered me a desk job, but I couldn't do it. I couldn't imagine just sitting there day after day, punching a keyboard, answering phones. I left the force and they gave me a pension settlement.

Tanja: Which, like an idiot, he immediately used as a down payment on our house.

Joe: Absolutely. I was starting a family. It was either buy a house while I could, or just wait for that money to trickle away and have nothing.

Tanja: I suppose you did the right thing, but you could have asked me first.

Joe: Isn't that just like a woman? She wants the man to take control, but when he does, she just wants to complain about it.

Tanja: That's right. It's my prerogative to complain about anything I want.

Joe rolls his eyes and leans back in the chair, crossing his arms over his chest. One doesn't need to be a master of body language to see where the interview is headed.

Mary: So that was when the two of you decided to start the agency?

Tanja: Not exactly. I was still working with the Bureau, but Joe didn't like that. He said it was dangerous, and he didn't like me being gone for days or weeks at a stretch.

Joe: There's no point getting married if you're going to be apart all the time. Besides, she was pregnant...

Tanja: I think the point my husband is so tactlessly trying to express is that long distance relationships can be difficult. After all, that is essentially what we had. And he's right. I didn't like being away from home so often, and I certainly couldn't continue working in the field with the baby coming.

I quit, but that left us in a bad financial situation. Joe had used most of his pension as the down payment for the house. I had some money saved up, but it wasn't a lot. Neither of us had experience in anything other than law enforcement, so the detective agency seemed like the next reasonable step.

Joe: Not that we thought of it ourselves.

Tanja: No, that's true. A friend of ours actually made the suggestion.

Mary: What friend?

Tanja: Sheriff Bill Diekmann. He's known Joe's family for decades, and he offered to give us some work.

Mary: You mean police work?

Tanja: Yes, the sheriff had a number of cold cases that he wanted us to investigate. He agreed to pay us out of a special fund for consultants, but only if we could solve the cases.

Mary: That sounds like you were under a lot of pressure. Did you have any luck?

Tanja: Thankfully, yes. In fact, we just closed one of the cases.

Mary: Fascinating. Would you care to tell me about it?

Tanja: (smiles and gets a distant look in her eyes) It was a sunny January morning, and I had just started a pot of coffee when I heard the doorbell ring...

*

Thanks for reading! If you enjoyed this book, please post a review at Amazon or your favorite online retailer, and remember to tell a friend!

Also, visit my website (www.jeramygates.com) and sign up for my newsletter for updates, giveaways, and Free Books!

16444948R00126

Printed in Poland
by Amazon Fulfillment
Poland Sp. z o.o., Wrocław